INTO THE HEART OF HELL

Sam Knight

ONE

Blaze awoke in a cold-sweat panic. There was something wrong in his apartment. No light came in through the windows; no glow came from his alarm clock.

Must be a power outage, he thought.

Wind howled outside, sucking at the windows, bowing them outward and then in again. Clattering sounds echoed faintly in the night. Maybe a soda can tumbling down the sidewalk.

Suddenly too hot to breathe, Blaze kicked off his covers. The disorientation of sleep faded and he came into focus.

There was something wrong in his apartment.

Listening, he slipped out of bed and crept to the threshold of his bedroom. Something was out there, in the hallway, waiting in the dark.

The back of his neck prickled and Blaze suddenly felt naked in his underwear. Scooping jeans off the floor, he kept watch on the doorway as he pulled them on. He fumbled in his nightstand drawer for the elastic headband with the LED light and turned it on. The light was weak and pitiful against the murky darkness. He grabbed his walking pole and held it ready, wishing it was a baseball bat.

Peeking into the hallway, he could sense the intruder, but his light revealed nothing. A whiff of a foul stink teased his nose. Sour milk. Banana peel. Cat shit.

Movement in the darkness caught his eye and he stopped, watching to see it again.

More shadows moved just outside of his beam of light. The curtains, maybe.

The wind beat against the apartment building, shaking it beneath Blaze's feet, adding to his unease. He stalked into the living room. A black shadow darted along the back wall and vanished.

The wind stopped.

Blaze felt the skin on his skull tighten. Goosebumps ran up and down his bare arms. There was nothing he could see, but he sensed movement and felt eyes on him.

"Who's there?" His voice sounded reedy to his own ears.

Distant, quiet laughter answered. An ambient sound, almost below his ability to hear, the quiet, baritone laugh filled the darkness, yet left Blaze wondering if he were imagining it.

Shaking with fear, Blaze spun in a circle, trying to make out more of the room than was revealed in the light from his headlamp. He made a slice through the air with his walking pole, then turned and did it again, testing to make sure nothing was behind him. Shadows flickered all around.

"Daniel…" A voice hissed within the sound of the laughter.

Blaze froze, waving his light frantically. "Who's there?" He choked on the words, steadied himself and then demanded forcefully, "Who are you?"

"Daniel…" The laughter stopped, leaving the world strangely empty and silent. Then the voice spoke clearly. "It is time, Daniel. I have come for you."

A door that had never been there before opened at the end of the hall, bathing the apartment in an unholy crimson light. Black shadows spilled out, dancing across the red-lit walls of the hallway, some spidery, some humanoid, none human. They surrounded Blaze, and one reached outward, taking corporeal form, and shoved at Blaze's shoulder.

Blaze stumbled and then fell, sprawling wildly and floundering in his panic. He slapped and kicked at the inhuman things around him as they pressed at his body, pushing him down the hallway toward the open door. The floor became slimy, and he began to slide as the demons shoved at him. Out of control, he gained speed as the floor tilted to an angle, sliding him down toward the gaping maw of Hell.

He screamed as his body fell into the open doorway. Flailing, he caught the doorframe with one hand as his body passed through. Desperately hanging on, he found himself dangling over a bottomless pit containing a blazing red sun. The cold of the blackness around him bit at his bare arms, chest, and feet. Even as the radiation from the inferno below began to burn him, frost formed on the side of his body facing away from it.

The laughter began again, this time it was a deep rumbling from somewhere in the direction of the burning light below. "Welcome, Daniel."

Blaze's fingers began to slip as he fought to hold on, to reach the doorframe with his other hand.

Please, God..., he silently prayed, unable to take a breath in the airless void.

The door slammed close, banging down against his fingers, numbing them with pain, trying to make him let go.

God. Please help me...

TWO

Blaze took a deep breath and tried to shake off the dream. Something was banging outside in the wind. A trashcan lid maybe. Loud enough to wake him and steady enough to give him dreams. He glanced at the alarm clock. It was two in the morning. Throwing back the covers, he stumbled to the bathroom, relieved himself, and drank some water. He stared into the mirror for a moment, not really seeing himself at all, but just being grateful for the feeling of normalcy.

Then he heard it. A quiet mewling sound.

He cocked his head, trying to hear it better over the banging noise and the moaning wind. A kitten? He followed the sound to the sliding glass door on his balcony. Seeing nothing, Blaze opened the door into the night.

The cold gale washed over him, sending shivers down his body. The sound was louder now, and it wasn't a kitten. It was a girl.

He could see her in the next apartment building, across the grassy common area, and a floor lower than his. A large tree branch had snapped and broken through her window as it fell. There were glass shards on the floor around her bare feet as she sat on her bed, wrapped in a nightshirt, sobbing.

Blaze looked down at her for a moment, then went back inside and shut the door. He had never seen her before, but that wasn't surprising. He hardly knew any of his neighbors. He'd only been here for a couple of months.

Taking a job in a new city had been like starting a whole new life, which was exactly what Blaze had wanted. His parents had been killed shortly after he graduated college, and, well, after settling out their estate and dealing with all the bills, he had needed a fresh start. There hadn't been anything left of his old life but memories anyway.

He pulled on his jeans, rummaged through the dirty laundry for a clean-ish t-shirt, and put on his shoes. He grabbed duct tape from the mess drawer in the kitchen, pulled a couple of trash bags out from under the sink, grabbed his keys, and accidentally kicked the headlamp lying on the floor.

Blaze stopped and looked down at the LED light.

Chills raced across his arms as he remembered taking it out of the nightstand drawer and coming out of the bedroom—in a dream. He swallowed hard, wondering how it had *actually* gotten here.

Looking around, with the lights on, everything in his apartment seemed normal. He peered back down the hall to where the nonexistent door had once been. Or had never been at all.

Picking up the headlamp, he tested it. It worked perfectly. Much brighter than it had been in the dream.

Dream? Or power outage? Had he been so tired he had walked around in a dream? Sleepwalked?

Shoving the light into his pocket, he walked slowly down the hallway, remembering how slippery the floor had felt, how it had tilted up to dump him out. He kneeled and touched the carpeting, running his fingers across the short pile, knowing it was irrational, but searching for any sign that it had been slimy.

The sound of the girl's crying caught his attention again. Blaze stood up and turned his back on his imaginary fears.

THREE

"Hello?" The girl's muffled voice was soft and uncertain from behind the closed door to her apartment.

"Hi. I'm Blaze. I live across the way, in the other building over there, third floor apartment with the lights on. I, uh, saw what the tree did to your window, and I came to help." Blaze held up the trash bags and duct tape for her to see through the peephole.

"Oh. Um… Just a minute."

After a moment he heard the rattle of locks, and she opened the door.

Her eyes were red rimmed from crying. Her blonde hair was disheveled and tangled, making the dark roots stand out. She smiled thinly at him as she dabbed at her nose with a crumpled tissue. She looked to be in her twenties, probably close to Blaze's own age, but in her jeans, oversized nightshirt, and striped red socks, he thought she could have passed for a kid who had just lost an argument with her parents.

"Hi." She did a quick, nervous wave with the tissue hand. "I'm Steph. I… Thank you for coming to help. I was kind of lost as to what to do."

"I was up anyway." Blaze realized his own hair was probably suffering from a serious case of bedhead. He hoped not. On a bad day, if he had been a redhead instead of a blond, he could have passed for Larry from the Three Stooges. Not the impression he liked to give. "The wind was pretty bad. Kind of gave me nightmares."

A haunted look came into Steph's eyes as he mentioned nightmares, and she nervously glanced around.

"You okay?" Blaze asked.

"Yeah." She took a breath and shook off the stress visible on her face. "Yeah. Come on in." Steph waved him into the room. "Sorry about the mess." She tried to smile but it looked more like a wince.

Blaze wiped his feet on the mat and stepped in.

Steph's apartment wasn't any warmer than the chill autumn air outside. She closed the door and rubbed her arms with her hands as he turned to look back at her.

"Let's cover up that window and see if we can get it warmer in here," he suggested.

Steph nodded and led him into her bedroom. The tree branch, sticking three feet into the room and dangling out the window, rocked back and forth in the wind, sweeping back and forth across the room like a giant clawed hand. Broken glass covered her bed, the floor, and the dresser.

"Wow! I can't believe you didn't get cut." Blaze stopped and looked at her again. "You are okay, aren't you?"

Steph nodded, but tears welled up in her eyes as she hugged herself tighter.

"Don't worry. We'll clean this up. And if you're not hurt, there's no real damage done, right? Everything else can be fixed."

She nodded again but did not seem convinced.

Blaze examined the tree branch, trying to figure out the best way to get it out of the window. He was testing how heavy the tree branch was when Steph blurted out, "It wasn't a tree."

"What?" He looked up at her.

With a quick, shaky hand movement, she pointed at the branch. "When that came through the window, it wasn't a tree."

A snapping noise came from outside, and the tree branch twisted and began falling out of the window, slashing Blaze across the cheek and catching on his t-shirt as it went. Steph screamed. The scraggly limb snagged on his shirt, dragging Blaze toward the window, trying to pull him out with it.

Blaze fought the weight tugging at him, grabbing at the bed, and then the floor, and finally at the windowsill itself, trying not to be yanked out into the night. He gasped for air as his shirt collar choked him, the weight of the tree limb dragging him halfway out through the window. Then his shirt ripped free from the branch's grasp, spinning him around as it tore.

The tree limb disappeared out of the window, scraping all the way down the side of the building like screams falling away into the pits of Hell.

Blaze gasped, looking down at the twenty-foot drop as the limb hit the ground and shattered into a small explosion of dead twigs and dried leaves.

"Oh my God! Are you all right?" Steph rushed over to Blaze and put her hand on his shoulder.

"Yeah. I'm okay." His face stung hotly, his back and arm burned from the scrapes.

"Ew. That's a nasty cut on your cheek. I'm so sorry."

Blaze put a hand to his face, and it came away wet with blood.

Steph turned and pulled some clean tissues out of the box by her bed and handed them to him. "Come on. Let's clean that up." She headed for the bathroom and he followed.

"Sit." She pointed to the closed toilet.

Blaze sat, feeling uncomfortable about having invaded this girl's personal space. He watched her dig through the medicine cabinet, taking out cotton balls and hydrogen peroxide.

"It's not that bad." He stood up. "Don't worry about it."

She put a hand on his shoulder and looked him in the eyes. "It is that bad. Sit down. I'll clean it for you."

He flinched when the soaked cotton ball dabbed at his cheek. He could hear the peroxide foaming in the cut.

"Looks like there's still something in there." Steph grabbed a pair of tweezers and leaned close.

Blaze could smell her. She smelled warm, comforting, and real. No perfumes. Her brown eyes caught his as she looked up from the wound, and he felt himself flush. She certainly did not remind him of a little girl anymore.

"Not too bad." She held up a splinter a quarter inch long. "But I think you should go see a doctor tomorrow, or you'll end up with a scar." She dropped the bloody piece of wood into the trash can and he heard it hit with a dull tink.

He looked at the wall, trying not to stare at her as she put a bandage on his cheek.

"That should keep the infection out, anyway."

Blaze nodded and stood up, not sure what to say and uncomfortable with the attraction he was feeling for her.

"Wait. Turn around. Let me see." Steph put her hand on his arm and spun him. She lifted the back of his shirt so she could see where the branch had scraped him. "These are a lot bigger, but not as bad. Makes you look like a skater." She pulled at his shirt, lifting it all the way up to his neck so she could clean the scratches.

Staring at her shower curtain, an abstract pattern of colored shapes on black, he felt like he was dangling over the abyss again, feeling the radiation burning his skin. Except the hot spots were where her hands brushed his skin as she cleaned the scrapes.

"This one might need a bandage, too," she told him and put one in the middle of his back. "All done." She let his shirt drop back into place.

"Thank you," he murmured. He moved around her, being careful not to brush up against her as she put things back into the medicine cabinet. Grabbing the duct tape and trash bags, he began sealing the shattered window. Small shards of glass crunched under his feet as he taped a trash bag onto the wall around the window frame. Oddly, the room seemed brighter with the black plastic covering the window and blocking out the night.

"It's warmer in here already. Thank you." Steph came back into the room.

"What were you saying, just before the tree…before I got cut?" Blaze asked her. "About it not being a tree?"

Steph looked away. "Nothing. It was stupid. I just had a nightmare." She grabbed a small plastic trashcan from the side of the bed and began putting broken glass in it. "Like you said. The wind was giving me nightmares. I just freaked when the window broke."

"I can't say that I blame you."

Blaze joined her in cleaning the mess, and they worked in silence as he thought about his own nightmare.

"Thank you again," Steph said as Blaze dumped the last of the glass into her kitchen trashcan. "I'm really sorry you got hurt."

"You're welcome." He smiled at her awkwardly for a moment then stepped toward the door.

"Blaze?"

"Yeah?"

Steph looked shyly at the ground before meeting his eyes. "Can I ask another favor? I mean, I know you've already done a lot for me, too much really, but…"

"Sure. What is it?"

She chewed nervously at her bottom lip. "Honestly, I'm just scared. The nightmare, and then the tree, really freaked me out. Could you keep me company, just until morning?" She looked anxious and then quickly added, "We could watch television, or talk. Or we don't even have to talk. If you are tired you could sleep on the couch. Or my bed. I'll sleep on the couch. I—I just really don't want to be alone."

Blaze looked at her pleading eyes and her worried face, and his heart nearly broke. She looked so vulnerable and afraid.

"Yeah, I'll stay."

FOUR

"So, you want to talk about your nightmare?" Blaze asked as he took a drink of the diet cola Steph had poured for him.

She sat in the large round papasan chair with her legs curled under her, sipping her own soda. "No," she shook her head. "Yes. I don't know. It was just…so real. There was this monster. I don't know what it was, but it kept calling my name and telling me it had come for me. Right when it was going to grab me, the tree broke the window and scared the crap out of me. Stupid, right?"

Blaze shook his head. "No. Stupid is when the monster doesn't even know your name. Mine kept calling me Daniel."

"Yours?"

"Yeah. My nightmare tonight. Someone was after me. They kept calling me by the wrong name."

Steph leaned closer. "How freaky is that? We both had the same dream on the same night!"

"Nah. My dream had this big black bottomless pit I was trying not to fall into. No monster chasing me."

"I've had dreams like that," Steph looked into her drink. "But only there is a big red sun down there waiting to burn me up and things are usually trying to push me into the hole."

Blaze's throat tightened at her words.

"Sorry." She looked up sheepishly. "It's silly I know. Dreams don't really mean anything. They just seem so real sometimes."

"No!" Blaze tried to calm his racing mind. "That was exactly my dream!"

Steph smiled, laughing and looking to the ceiling. "Now you're trying to freak me out. Pretty soon we'll break out the Ouija board and the scary movies, next thing you know, we'll be cuddling in the dark, right?"

"No, that really was my dream. I'm kind of creeped out right now myself."

The room suddenly went black. Blaze heard Steph take a sharp breath of air in surprise.

"Don't worry, Steph. It's just the storm. It'll come back on it just a minute. The power went out earlier, too."

"No it didn't."

"What?"

"My clocks were all the right time. If the power went off earlier, I would've had to re-set them."

Blaze felt fear begin to crawl across his skin as he realized his clock had been right, too. The blackout had been part of the dream. But then why had the headlamp been on the floor?

He remembered the headlamp was in his pocket, and he pulled it out, thumbing the button on. The red map light filled the room, and Steph screamed.

Dark figures surrounded her. The same willowy inhuman shadows that had been on the wall of Blaze's hallway now seethed in the darkness around them, writhing to stay out of the light.

"No!" Blaze jumped up, spilling his soda. He threw the glass at the nearest shadow, but the glass vanished just as it should have impacted.

Steph screamed again and again as the things grabbed at her, dragging her out of the chair by her arms, legs, and hair.

"Help!" Steph screeched, unable to stop the terrors from taking her. A spidery shadow ran up her chest and clamped itself over her face, muffling her screams.

Blaze leaped after her, but something mired his feet, tripping him and holding him down. Another spidery black shadow flickered around his ankles, circling his legs. Blaze kicked at it, but it was like kicking at taffy. He tried to grab it, pull it off his feet, but he couldn't seem to get hold of it.

Then the thing grabbed back at Blaze, catching the hand holding the headlamp. The little monster wrapped itself around his fist, enveloping the light and sending the room back into blackness.

Panicked, Blaze punched the floor, trying to dislodge the creature around his hand. He could still feel the light in his grasp, under the tar-like substance of the spider-thing.

A different red light filled the room. A familiar, radiating light Blaze had never wanted to see again. A door opened where Steph's television should have been, and the gaping pit from Blaze's nightmare stood before him again.

Silhouetted in the ruddy light, Steph struggled in the grip of the shadowy demons as they pulled her toward the doorway. The red light of Hell reflected in the whites of her terrified eyes as she screamed for Blaze to help her.

"No! No!" Blaze ignored the thing wrapped around his fist and lunged after Steph. He grabbed at the closest demon, catching an insubstantial handful of shadow that dissipated in his grasp. He lunged again and caught Steph's foot just as she was pulled through the doorway.

She left the gravity of the normal world and was pulled forward, her weight jerking and pulling hard at Blaze's shoulder as she fell straight away from him, yet down toward the pit in front of them. Blaze scrabbled at the doorframe with his other hand, losing the headlamp and the creature holding it as he did.

His body was being slowly dragged in after her.

"Don't drop me!" Steph screamed. The shadow things were gone now, but she was being pulled away from him by the force of an unholy gravity. "Blaze! Please don't drop me!"

Hanging out over the void, Blaze grimaced as he tried to hook his legs on something, anything to anchor himself in the world on his side of the door so he could grab Steph with both hands.

"Blaze! Please!"

He looked down at the girl clinging to his hand and then past her, into the red sun radiating hate up at them. The laughter from his nightmare began again. A quiet rumble at first, growing into a raucous roar. Then came the voice.

"Daniel…" It was a terrible voice, deep and penetrating.

Steph continued to scream, trying to bend her torso enough to grab hold of his arm with her hands. Blaze tried to pull back but could not. Her struggles caused her to swing, pulling on his arm even more.

Blaze fought back tears of rage and frustration. He didn't have enough strength to pull her up.

"Daniel…"

Straining his whole body, Blaze roared in a final effort to bring her back in through the door, but he couldn't do it. He couldn't pull her in and he couldn't hold on. His grip slipped as sweat formed between his hand and her ankle. His own body continued to slide, inexorably, through the Hellish doorway.

"Please don't let go of me!" Steph's plea came as her foot slipped beyond Blaze's ability to hold on to both her and the door.

Blaze closed his eyes and released his grip on the last part of the sane world he could still touch.

As they fell through the door, dropping through the void toward the red sun, Blaze pulled Steph close to him, held her tight, and tried to protect her from the fall, from her own screaming, and from the voice that now encompassed everything.

"Daniel…You came to Me."

FIVE

Blaze floated, alone, in a vast nothingness. Confused, he looked around. There was nothing. Everywhere there was nothing. He waved his arms and kicked his feet, but he had no sense of movement, no up or down. Nothing.

How long had he been here? It felt like he had been here for a very long time. Forever, perhaps. Yet, he had just been falling toward the red sun, holding Steph.

He floated in the nothingness, unable to do anything else. Time passed. Or did not. He couldn't tell. Eventually he felt a presence with him. An enormous all-encompassing presence, all around him.

"Welcome, Daniel." The voice resonated through his skull. More than that. It permeated his entire being. He heard it with something other than his ears, something he had never heard with before.

"My name's not Daniel." He spoke, but the words did not go anywhere in the void. They felt muffled and dead, as though he were in a soundproofed room, and they didn't seem to have come from his mouth.

"Just because you do not think your name is Daniel, does not mean it is not. Blaze may be the name your surrogate parents called you by, but Daniel is the name your mother emblazoned upon your soul."

As the words were spoken, Blaze felt truth in them. He felt the certainty of them vibrate through his being so strongly he couldn't imagine denying it was so. His parents, the people who had loved him, raised him, given him everything, were not his birth parents. The revelation stunned him. He felt as though he had always known this, somehow, deep in his soul, although he knew he had just learned it.

Laughter filled the void. "Or should I say *My* soul?"

Understanding came instantly with those final words. He was speaking with Satan, and Satan had claimed his soul.

Blaze cowed, weeping with the sadness of an empty heart and uncontrollable fear.

SIX

Steph screamed as she fell away from him, spinning out into the void, sucked down toward the red star. Blaze watched in horror, unable catch her. How had she slipped from his arms? How had he gotten back here from the nothingness? Unable to make himself fall faster and catch up with her, all he could do was flail uselessly and watch in horror as she shrank away from him.

Screaming for his help, she fell into the inferno until, flames sprouting from her body, she burned up. And then she was gone.

The horrible laughter echoed all through the void around him.

The Hellish door vanished and Blaze found himself lying on the floor of Steph's apartment, alone. He sat up and looked around. His soda glass was upturned in a wet spot on the rug. Everything else was quiet and... normal.

"Steph?" He got up and began walking through the apartment. A sick feeling in his stomach told him he wouldn't find her, but he had to try anyway. "Steph?"

Someone pounded on the front door, startling him. Blaze looked at the door. Should he answer it? It wasn't his apartment.

"Police!" A muffled voice called through the door before the pounding began again.

Shakily, Blaze answered the door.

"We received a call for a domestic disturbance," a female officer said, craning her neck to see into the apartment behind him as he opened the door.

"May we come in?" her male counterpart asked. It wasn't really a question.

Blaze stepped aside and held the door open.

"Do you live here?" the woman asked as she entered, scanning the room. Her eyes instantly fell on the soda glass.

"No," Blaze choked out on his second attempt.

"Who does?" the male policeman asked.

"S-Steph."

"Where is Steph?" he asked, as his partner continued to poke her head into rooms.

"I…" Blaze didn't know what to say. How could he tell them she had just been dragged through a door to Hell by shadow demons?

"Where is Steph?" The policeman repeated the question, watching Blaze intently.

"I was just trying to find her," Blaze finally answered.

"You don't know where she is?"

Blaze shook his head.

"Who are you?"

Blaze told him. "I live over there, in the next building." He pointed lamely in the general direction.

"Does Steph let you come in whenever you want?"

"What? No. I mean, this is the first time I have ever been here. I just met her."

"You just met Steph, and you are alone in her home at three in the morning?"

Blaze felt panicked, accused. He stuttered as he tried to give his explanation. "The windstorm…The tree broke her window. She was crying, so I came over and put up the plastic on the window and helped her pick up the glass. But now she's…she's gone." The words felt final as he said them. She was gone.

"Gone where? Where did Steph go?"

"I—I don't know. She was just here and… now she's not." That was as close to the truth as he could bring himself to say.

"There's no one else here," the female officer reported as she came back into the room. "Bedroom window has been broken, taped up with black plastic."

"That's what I was doing," Blaze nodded. "I was helping her clean that up."

"Do you have an ID on you?" the male officer asked Blaze.

"No. It's back at my apartment."

"Let's go get it."

Blaze's apartment lights were still on when he unlocked the door and let the officer in.

"Tell me again how you came to be over there," the officer demanded as he looked at Blaze's ID.

"The windstorm made a bunch of noise, woke me up. Then I heard crying. When I came out here to see what it was," Blaze opened the sliding glass door and went out on the balcony, "I could see her down there." He pointed at the window he had covered with the trash bag. "That tree branch, on the ground there, had broken her window, and she was sitting on the bed, crying."

The outlines of Steph's room could barely be made out through the nearly opaque trash bags.

"And you just thought you would go over there and help?" The officer asked as he wrote notes down on a little pocket notepad.

"Well…yeah. She looked really upset."

"And you didn't know her before this?"

"No."

"What was she wearing?"

Blaze thought about it for a moment. "When I looked down there, she was sitting on her bed wearing a long nightshirt. One of the fuzzy ones with a cartoon character on it. BlueBug, I think."

"You could tell that from here?"

"I don't remember. I just remember from when I saw her wearing it over there. When I got there, she had put on a pair of jeans."

"Was she wearing any shoes?"

"No. She had those socks with the gripper things on the bottoms. Red and white striped socks."

The officer's cell phone rang. He stepped off the balcony and back into the apartment, a little ways away from Blaze for privacy, yet kept his eyes on him. After a moment he pulled the phone away from his cheek and asked, "What is the blood in the bathroom?"

Blaze frowned, feeling a panic that he would be accused of something even more than the break-in he was starting to worry about. Then he remembered his cheek. "This." He pointed to the bandage on his cheek.

"The tree branch was still sticking in the window, and when I tried to push it out, it cut me. That's what tore my shirt, too." He turned around and showed it to the officer. He had forgotten about his torn shirt. What had they been thinking when they saw him? He must have looked like someone who had broken in and attacked Steph. Did they think he had done something to her?

The officer repeated Blaze's answer into his cell phone, listened a moment, and then asked, "Would you please lift your shirt? I would like you see your back."

Blaze complied, lifting it up as best as he could.

"Who put the bandage on your back?"

"Steph did." Blaze futilely tried to look over his own shoulder to see the bandage in the middle of his back. "She cleaned the scrapes up for me and then we cleaned up all of the glass."

The officer said something into his phone and then hung it up. "And then what happened?"

Blaze swallowed hard. He had been dreading that question. "And then she told me she was still scared and asked me to stay until the sun came up." The officer's face kept a professional affect, but Blaze felt the implied impropriety burn on his face anyway. "It wasn't like that." He tried to defend himself. "She really was scared. She asked me if I wanted a soda, and then we sat down in the living room and talked."

The police officer nodded as he wrote. "And then?"

Blaze didn't know what to say. He couldn't tell them 'and then these shadow demons from a dream I had earlier tonight grabbed her and threw her through a magic door that led into a bottomless pit with a red sun blazing in the middle of it. I tried to grab her, but I couldn't hold on. Honest, that's what happened.' Instead, he lied. He felt terrible about it, but even as he told the lie, he realized it was likely the truth, as what seemed to be the truth made no sense at all.

"And then I must have fallen asleep. The next thing I knew, you guys were knocking on the door."

"And where did Steph go?"

"I don't know." That was kind of true. He really didn't know what or where the place Steph had gone to was.

The officer glanced at his wristwatch, which made Blaze habitually look to the clock on the wall. It was a little after four in the morning.

"Do you have to work today?" the officer asked.

"No. I'm off on Mondays."

"What's your phone number?"

Blaze gave it to him. The officer dialed it, and Blaze's cell phone rang. The officer hung up as Blaze pulled it out of his pocket to answer it.

"I'll be in touch later today," the officer told him as he handed Blaze his business card. "If you see Steph, or hear from her, I want to know. Immediately."

Blaze nodded and watched the officer walk out the door.

SEVEN

Tossing and turning in his bed, Blaze was unable to fall back asleep. What had happened to Steph? Had it all been a dream? It couldn't have been, or the police wouldn't have gotten involved. Things just made no sense at all.

He felt like he could still hear her kitten-like sobs, calling out plaintively through the night. Was it his fault? He'd had the nightmare before he went over to see her. Had he brought his nightmare to her? Had it taken her even though it had come for him? Why had it kept calling him Daniel? What about the nightmares Steph said she'd had?

Terrors and worries swirled in his mind as he feared for his sanity. It couldn't have happened the way he remembered, yet he couldn't bring himself to dismiss any of it. And what if she didn't turn up? Were the police going to think he killed her?

His stomach ached at the thought. Who would believe he was innocent if he tried to say what really happened? And how could he defend himself if he was there when she vanished? And where was Steph now?

She told him she'd had nightmares about the abyss with the red sun in it too. Did that mean it was real? Or was that part of the nightmare?

He buried his face into his hands. "Oh, my God! Am I going insane?" Blaze's head felt like it would explode with unanswered questions, with confusion, fear. And the unceasing sound of Steph's sobs.

He found himself with his hands over his ears, trying to block out the lamenting cries. He took his hands away from his head and sat up. He was hearing her cries again!

He had left lights on, so he could see everything, and his room looked normal, sane. But he could hear her. Crying.

He got out of bed, cocking his head to pinpoint the direction her cries came from. They sounded like they were somewhere *inside* his apartment.

Had she snuck over here somehow? Hidden from the police? He dismissed the thought as the hair on the back of his neck rose.

He knew where she had gone. She had gone into the abyss.

Stepping out into the hallway, Blaze froze at the sight of the door that did not belong there. It had returned to the end of his hallway.

It was open only a little, just a crack, but that horrible red light was seeping out around the edges, filling his hallway again. And so were the piteous sounds of Steph's misery.

He stepped forward, cautiously keeping an eye out for any inhuman shadows that might appear to try and force him through the door. But no shadows danced down the walls of his lighted hallway. Nothing approached or menaced him. There was only the door, slightly ajar, beckoning him. Daring him, defying him.

Edging back into his room, he took a deep breath and blew it out slowly. He peeked back out into the hall. The door was still there.

Blaze thought about calling the officers, telling them Steph was behind that door. Would they believe him? Would the door still be there by the time they got here? Or was this another nightmare, just a dream?

He pinched himself, praying he would wake up.

Steph's sobs broke and turned into a shriek of raw terror. The blood-freezing sound of someone screaming their throat raw, seeing the worst coming at them, trying to repel it with their voice.

Blaze shrank away from his bedroom doorway, his pulse pounding. He tripped over his shoes and fell backward, landing hard and crab-walking farther away from the horrible noise of what was surely Steph's demise. Her scream faltered, then came again, weaker, in pain. He heard words. She was pleading. He couldn't quite make out the words, but she was pleading. Pleading for her life, pleading for it to stop, pleading to die… Blaze couldn't tell what she was begging for, but it was horrid. Tears streamed down his face as he tried to cover his ears, tried not to hear.

"Steph!" he screamed. He couldn't take it anymore, he had to do something. He didn't know what was happening to her, but whatever it was, it shouldn't happen to anyone, ever.

He fumbled to put on the shoes he had tripped over. He grabbed his walking pole, grimaced through his tears, and tried not to vomit as he hoarsely whispered, "I'm coming Steph. I'm coming."

EIGHT

Blaze carefully reached out and touched the Hell door, afraid that it might actually burn him. It was cold but it felt like a normal door. He gently pulled, opening it wider to see inside. The stench of rotten garbage filled his apartment again and he gagged.

Steph's cries were weak, but continued on in agonizing misery.

Blaze expected to look down into the abyss again, expected he would have to turn back when faced with jumping down into the red sun, but instead, he found a hallway made of old hand-hewn stone blocks with slime dripping down them. The red light emanating from the door did not seem to come from the hallway, as the stone hall was dark and moist, lit by something like a green bioluminescence.

Steeling himself and holding the walking pole point out, Blaze stepped into the hallway, toward Steph's pleas.

The hot air washed over him, smelling of rot, mold and mildew, and he gasped in the thick atmosphere that seemed to hold little oxygen. The sound of a pebble dropping onto rock echoed through the hall and he spun around. His apartment was gone. The door was gone.

His world was gone.

The stone tunnel extended both ways for as far as he could see, the green glow allowing his eyes to follow the lines of the corridor to pinpoints on a tiny, confined horizon.

Steph's cries beckoned him, and he turned back the way he'd first started. He slipped in a puddle of slime, coating his hand with more of the gunk when he touched the wall to steady himself. He tried to wipe it off on a dry looking rock but only managed to collect more. He gave up and wiped his hand on his jeans. The slime balled and rolled, sticking to his hands and pants like rubber cement.

After that he was careful not to brush the walls. Each step collected more goo on the bottom of his shoes, making them squishy and causing him to slide to the left or to the right when he put his foot down. His makeshift weapon quickly became a walking stick again.

Trying not to lose his balance, Blaze almost didn't notice the peephole in the wall. A missing brick, about the size and shape of a candy bar. A slight yellow light emanated from it. He peered in.

Inside was a giant ball of snakes—no not snakes. Worms. *Mealworms?* Blaze grimaced as he looked at mealworms the size of humans, twisting into each other, forming a roughly spherical shape, squirming and writhing in the middle of a small stone room. A sickly yellow glow came from everywhere, yet from nowhere. An opening appeared in the ball as the worms made a gap, seemingly just for Blaze to see into.

In the middle of the ball was a naked man. He was screaming. No sound came out, but Blaze could see him screaming. The worms wriggled around the man's naked legs, arms and across his back. The sharp, stumpy little legs of the larval insects clawed the man for purchase as they grabbed hold of him, pulled themselves along, and grabbed hold again. The man took another breath, a small wheezing sound Blaze could barely hear, and then began screaming again.

Blood flecks flew from the man's mouth as he screamed, but no sound came. His voice was gone, ruined forever from the screams, but he screamed on nonetheless. He screamed on, and the mealworms continued to grab him with their sharp little claws and drag their giant, plump, yellow ringed bodies across his naked skin.

Blaze fell back away from the peephole, sitting down hard into the slime puddles.

For the first time, Blaze truly realized where he was. He was in Hell.

Steph's screams had become weaker. Was she covered in worms too? How long until she screamed her voice away? He wouldn't be able to find her if that happened.

He slipped in the goo as he used the walking stick to stand. Climbing to his feet, he started off in a careful, plodding jog toward the sound of her voice. He passed other peepholes with various colored glows emanating from them. Blue, yellow, red, purple, they all had some form of sickly, out of place, color coming from them in an unnatural way, as though he could see smells and emotions exuding outward. Blaze never stopped to look. He continued on, trying not to think of what horrors might lie within those cells.

Some had sounds coming from them. Sucking sounds, rending sounds, clawing, scraping, flatulent, slurping noises, and worse, spurred him on past without looking.

He couldn't tell if he was making any headway or not. Steph's screaming was still somewhere ahead of him, but it was growing weaker, making it hard to tell if he was getting closer. He raced on, determined to reach her before she couldn't scream anymore.

He tripped and fell, landing face-first into a puddle of muck. The stuff coated his face, covered his mouth and nose, threatening to suffocate him when it didn't come off. He clawed at the ooze, peeling and pushing it off his mouth until he could gasp for air again. It took him valuable moments to clear his eyes enough to see again.

Too many valuable moments. Steph's voice went hoarse as he stumbled on. It went hoarse, and then he couldn't hear it anymore.

NINE

Blaze continued on, checking each peephole he passed, checking to see if Steph was behind it. Each viewport revealed something worse than the last. He vomited in revulsion and horror after the second one he looked into, but he continued on. Some had one person in it, others had a few. One had a multitude, an entire auditorium of people who had their attention focused on a lone individual in the center.

Blaze expected the person in the center to be screaming silently, but she was…complacent. Her face was sad, accepting. It was the people in the auditorium, chained to their seats, who had screamed their throats away watching the woman slowly be consumed by lava from the ankles up. The smell followed him away from the viewport.

As he staggered on, Blaze became aware of another sound, one that had been there for a while, but he hadn't noticed until now. His own sobbing. His own ragged breath through the tears and snot streaming down his face.

He tried not to think about it, tried not to think about the horrors around him. He pushed on, looking for Steph. That was all that mattered right now. She needed him. There was no one else in the world coming to help her. It all depended upon him.

He fell again and sobbed into his hands. What was he doing? How could he do this? He was trying to rescue someone from Hell? He was in Hell!

How do you get out of Hell? Maybe he should be more worried about getting himself out.

He looked back the way had come. The stony walls extended forever, as far as he could tell. And they all looked the same. How far had he come? A mile? Maybe. Maybe only a hundred yards. Maybe forever.

Time had no meaning in this place. Only terror, remorse, regret, and self-loathing seemed to mean anything. He was lost.

Somewhere he'd lost his walking stick and hadn't even noticed. He got up and began to move forward. There was nothing else to do.

A peephole that somehow glowed black revealed a man eating his own feet. A purple one held a decapitated head rolling, wild-eyed, toward a headless body, yet never getting any closer.

More windows into Hell went by, but none of them contained Steph.

Exhausted, Blaze stopped at an orange glowing one and readied himself to witness yet another horror. When he looked in his stomach turned.

A madman stomped and kicked at babies barely old enough to crawl. The babies cried and wailed. They died horribly, with squeals of pain and bubbling blood in their mouths, as the man killed them, but more kept appearing. He picked one up and used it to bash in the head of another. He used it until its leg ripped free and its body was flung from his hand.

Blaze vomited again. After all the things he had seen, he hadn't thought any could get worse, but they did.

"Stop it!" he screamed at the man. "Stop it!"

The man continued beating the infants to death, slipping on blood, and worse, while kicking dead ones out of the way, trying to make room for himself to stand.

Blaze pounded his fists on the wall. "Stop!" A small stone came loose and fell by Blaze's feet. He picked it up and hurled it through the peephole. With an unerring accuracy that shocked Blaze, the stone hit the man in the eye in an explosion of blood.

The man staggered, surprised by something, anything, different happening in his private Hell. He stopped killing babies and held a hand over his ruined eye. A strange smile grew on his face. He spotted the rock and picked it up, entranced by the novel thing.

Then the first baby took a bite out of his leg. Razor sharp teeth took a chunk out the size of a quarter. The man screamed hoarsely, as though it was the first sound he had made in a century. Another baby bit into him, and another.

The man kicked them away, but more were on top of him, biting at him. One bit into his Achilles tendon at his ankle and he fell to one knee. The fumbling babies took more bites as the man fought to clear them away from him, but the break in his attack was all they had needed to overwhelm him. Soon he was buried under bloody-mouthed infants feasting upon his flesh.

Blaze collapsed against the wall, stunned. Not only from the sight of yet another horror, but with the knowledge that he had added to this one.

"Good on ya!" The words startled Blaze. "The Boss was a bit irritated that he had managed to hold them off for so long this time!" High pitched and whiney, but with an Australian accent, the voice seemed cartoonish, out of place, even here, where nothing was right.

Blaze looked for the source of the voice and found a platypus, sitting up like a prairie dog at his feet. Reflexively, he kicked at it, expecting something in this place to bite at him, or breathe fire, or vomit Easter bunnies. He missed.

The creature was quick and dodged easily. "Missed me, missed me, now you gotta kiss me!" it said in a voice like Bugs Bunny. Then it leaped at his face.

Blaze threw his hands up, but by the time the creature landed it had grown in size and changed shape into something resembling a squid. The weight of the thing bore Blaze down to the ground as it suctioned onto his face. Something like a tentacle with suckers on it forced its way into Blaze's mouth and down his throat, gagging him.

The tentacle pulled out in a sudden jerk, leaving Blaze retching and gasping for air.

"Don't make me wanna kiss you again." The thing looked like an octopus with an hourglass figure as it talked in a Mae West impersonation. "Next time, I might not be able to control myself, Big Boy."

Blaze tried to scurry away, but the creature was already ahead of him, now in the shape of a mule chomping on a cigar. "I know what yer thinkin'." The voice was deep, gruff with a Bronx accent now. "Yer askin' yerself, 'How'd I get so lucky?' Most people get one little private Hell all their own they have ta be in forever, but me?" The mule winked conspiratorially. "And by me, I mean you." It switched its cigar to the other side of its long face with a quick motion of its big, pink tongue. "But me? I get a little of everyone's Hell! Can ya beat that with a stick?"

Blaze shook his head, not knowing what to say.

"Ah! A good audience! Everyone likes a good audience." The thing still chomped its cigar, but was now a Groucho Marx-like duck complete with a mustache, but it had Harpo and Chico's heads for feet. "Speaking of liking a good audience, you are nothing like one. But whaddaya expect? You're in Hell. Nothing's good here.

"But I digress…" The thing now stood large enough to fill the tunnel. It was a squid again. No, an octopus. No. It was worse. So much worse. The voice that emanated from it now sounded like an over-educated movie villain. Smooth, suave, and commanding. "The Boss has decreed that you are a bit, shall we say…special. He has machinations that involve you, and therefore you get the special treatment. Part of which…" The creature vanished.

"…is me." It appeared again on Blaze's shoulder the size of a bug. "You can think of me as your anti-Jiminy Cricket." It turned into a thing half-spider, half snail. "You see, I'm kind of the opposite of your conscious. I'm here to make things even worse for you in every way I can."

It appeared in front of him again, as a voluptuous woman with heaving breasts glistening with sweat. Blaze could smell the sexual arousal coming off of her as she leaned close and whispered. "But don't bother trying to give me a name. I don't have one. I don't need one."

Danny DeVito this time. "Because I'll be with you every fucking step of the way! I'm never going to leave your side! You'll never get away from me! Whaddaya think of that?"

Blaze swallowed. The whole thing had been so surreal his mind was spinning. "Well, thank God you've got a sense of humor."

Suddenly fire was burning the flesh off Blaze's bones. He could see the meat curling away from his arms and legs as he tried to scream, but the hot air seared his throat and blistered his lungs, charring them away. His eyes filmed over, cooking in the flames, and he could no longer see, only feel the pain. So much pain.

Slowly, agonizingly slowly, his body was put back together by ants wearing golf cleats. They trampled every tiny piece of flesh back into place with their cleats, and then stapled it on with their mandibles. It took at least a century for them to finish. By that time Blaze had all but gone mad from lack of mental stimulation. He had recited every math problem he could think of, he had tried to recreate every book he had ever read, every movie he had ever seen.

"Poor choice of words, there Daniel," Humphrey Bogart told him. "We don't have too many rules around here, see? But the ones we do got are strictly enforced."

Blaze looked around. He was back in the tunnel, with the shape-changing creature. The creature clicked its tongue as it turned into a little girl. "And that was less than a second," she sighed and held up a giant rainbow lollipop. She looked at it with big wistful blue eyes and shook her head sadly, bouncing her perfect golden curls. "The Boss took it easy on you. I think He likes you for some reason." Her eyes flared red and she screamed, flames shooting from her mouth. "Imagine what He does to someone who really pisses Him off!"

Blaze stepped backward to avoid being burned again.

"Now, where were we?" The thing turned into Rodney Dangerfield. "Oh yeah. You were going to keep wandering, lost in Hell, and I was going to torment you! Say… Did you mean it when you said I had a sense of humor? I could use a little respect."

TEN

Blaze walked on trying to ignore the creature. It refused to answer any direct questions but continued changing shape and performing antics between the comedic and the macabre, constantly tormenting him with hints about which cell Steph might be in. It heckled him each time he looked into another wrong one. When Blaze refused to pay attention to it, it bit him, or spit rancid custard on him, or blocked his path until he apologized. Finally, just to make sure Blaze would continue to pay attention to it, the creature ate a woman.

When Blaze had looked into her torture chamber, she had been getting poked with needles, in the eyes, by giant humanoid penises. When he ignored the creature's lewd comments, it slid a tentacle through the little peephole, grabbed the woman by the neck, and beat her head against the wall until the rocks broke away and it was able to pull her out through the hole. Then it proceeded to eat her, limb by limb, asking "You wanna ignore me now? How about now?" between bites.

"All right! I'm paying attention! Stop it!"

"Too little, too late." The creature continued eating, holding the woman's head close to its mouth so she could hear the crunching of her own bones. "Can't let a meal go to waste."

The woman tried to scream, but, of course, her throat was already ruined from screaming. By the time the creature bit her head off, it was a relief not to see the tortured look upon her face anymore.

"Please…please…" Blaze fell back against the wall and sunk to the floor, reduced to tears and blubbering again.

"It was the 'please' that caught my attention." The creature changed shaped into a masked man and struck a stately pose. "What was it you had to live for? Love? Twue wuv?"

"Please stop. Don't hurt anyone else…"

"Sleep well, Daniel, I'll most likely kill you in the morning." The creature looked down at Blaze and cracked a hideous smile that split far too wide across its face. "I always wanted to say that."

"What do you want from me?" Blaze held his face in his hands.

The creature's voice went droll. "I want a hamburger. No, cheeseburger. I want a hot dog. I want a milkshake. I want potato chips…" It fell silent.

Blaze looked up. It was staring expectantly at him.

"Seriously?" the creature asked, adjusting its cardigan in a very annoyed manner. "You can't do the next line? What's with kids these days? They think they're too good for the classics. Bet you could quote the fuck out of Lady GaGa though, couldn't you? I have to admit, it was tempting to eat her when she wrapped herself in bacon." Drool poured out from between the creature's teeth and cascaded from its lips.

"What do you want from me?" Blaze screamed in frustration.

"That's better, kid. Let it all out. You know it's no big secret." The creature leaned in close. "We just want your soul."

Blaze blanched.

"Actually, we've already got it. We just want you to come around to working with us on your own. Makes things easier that way."

Shakily, Blaze stood up. "Wh—what do you mean?"

"What do I mean when I say we've already got it? I mean your parents made a deal with the Boss when you were born. Actually, you weren't born yet, but details, details. Your parents sold your soul to the Devil, and now He owns you.

Now, isn't that special." The creature was a skinny old lady in a wig. "And not just your soul, your sister's too." It giggled.

"My sister…?"

"Oh yeah! The Boss went all Vader on you, baby!" Becoming a black cloaked and helmeted figure, it began breathing heavily. "A sister…you have…a sister. Now Obi Wan's failure is complete."

The demon majestically waved his hand and a door appeared in the middle of the hallway, looking just as it had in Blaze's apartment. "Go on. Open it."

Shakily, Blaze stood and put a hand on the door. It opened at his touch. Inside was Steph, playing poker, with some dogs. Tears ran down her face. She was mostly naked, wearing only one red striped sock and a pair of panties.

"Steph!" Blaze tried to run to her, but the air around him got thicker and thicker until he couldn't move any farther forward. "Steph!"

"No good. Can't hear you!" The creature was a monkey with hands over its ears. It moved to cover its eyes. "Can't see you either."

Blaze tried pounding on the barrier, but there was nothing solid enough to hit.

"She's wishing she'd dressed in layers for this one." Now a little kid bundled inside several parkas, the creature, barely able to walk, hobbled over to the roaring fire lighting the Victorian game room and rubbed its hands together in the warmth. "They're playing strip poker. After she runs out of clothes, they start taking body parts. The dogs really like winning bones."

The creature sighed and turned into a big scaly green demon. "Too bad for her she doesn't know how to play Dragon Strip Poker. You know, she's already lost at War, which was played with shuriken instead of cards, naturally. And she lost at Keno. Played with body parts. You bet them on the numbers that come up and try to win some back. So far she hasn't done very well, which is too bad. She doesn't seem to enjoy it much when they eat her, but she really, really hates it when they shit her out and put her back together again."

Blaze's lip curled in anger. This place was horrible. He stood up, gathering his strength, preparing to do something, anything.

"Ah! There's the spark the Boss saw! Go get 'em, Tiger!"

Angry at all of the jibes, Blaze turned back to the smart aleck creature, now looking like a cartoon tiger. The thing saw the look on his face and melted into a dark shadow, like the demons that had dragged Steph through the door.

"Ooooh! Whaddaya gonna do?" The demon hissed. "Hit me? Just remember what happened when you tried to kick me. Next time I'll go up your ass instead of down your throat. Unless you think you'd like that? I could go both ways. Meet in the middle. We could get *real* close." The creature leaned in and Blaze could smell its fetid breath over the rest of the disgusting odors of Hell.

It sneered at him and something inside of Blaze snapped. He grabbed the mocking creature by the throat and squeezed as hard as he could.

The creature's eyes went wide in surprise and then narrowed with anger. It squirmed, trying to break free of Blaze's grip, but seemed unable to loosen it. Blaze added his other hand to the choke hold. The demon changed shape into a hagfish and secreted globs of mucus all over Blaze's hands and wrists as it twisted its snake-like body into knots, but Blaze refused to let go.

The thing stopped squirming and began to grow.

It grew so large and heavy, Blaze fell to the ground with it, fighting to stay on top, trying not to get crushed, but refusing to let go. The area under his hands tried to expand, but Blaze squeezed harder and it was unable to break free of his grip. The creature swung a giant fist up at him, but Blaze dodged, rolling to one side, never releasing his hold.

Spiked tentacles grew out of the creature's sides, waving wildly in the air. They pulled back wide and then stabbed in hard, spearing Blaze through the arms, the legs, and his back.

He screamed in pain and buried his face into his arms, trying to protect himself without letting go of the creature's throat.

Then, true to its word, the creature attacked between Blaze's legs. Blaze gasped as the spiked tentacle shot up his anus, lifted him into the air, and began to twist.

Shaking, but still holding his grip, Blaze looked the creature in the eyes. "Fuck you," he gritted through clenched teeth, refusing to die without taking the demon with him. "Fuck you!" With a final effort, Blaze squeezed, twisted, and pulled the creature's head off its neck.

The tentacled body stiffened and turned hard, freezing in place like a statue, with Blaze impaled upon it, feet dangling above the ground.

Knowing he was dying, Blaze held the still-squishy head up and looked into the slit-shaped, goatish eyes that were still wildly looking around. "Fuck you." Blaze spit blood into the eyes. He roared in anger and stabbed his fingers into one of the eyes, reaching into the socket and ripping the orb out.

Ichor dripping from his hand, Blaze lost his strength and began to go limp as he hung impaled.

At some point his struggle had caught the attention of the dogs playing poker with Steph, although she still seemed oblivious to his presence. Weakly, he threw the eye at one of the dogs. A mouth, on the end of a tentacle, shot up from the top of the dog's head and snapped the eye out of the air.

A hysterical giggle escaped Blaze's bloody lips. "Now that's fucking funny."

Blaze pulled the other eye out and threw it at another dog. He missed, and two of the dogs leaped from the table to fight over the eye. Steph didn't notice. "Funny… Ha Ha… funny," Blaze mumbled. "I'll show you something funny." He stuck his fist back into the head and felt around, singing, "…if you only had a brain…"

Inside the head, he found something small and hard. He pulled it out and threw the limp, floppy head aside like an empty, wet trash bag. Unclenching his fist, he found a small black crystal, with smoky darkness swirling around inside of it. The thing radiated an unholy energy that Blaze knew was the demon's true form.

"I got you…" Blaze gasped. "How you like me now?"

Struggling to find purchase for his feet on the spikes of the tentacle that had impaled him, he slowly pushed himself upward, sliding himself up inch by inch, screaming in pain as the hooks and barbs in it caught at his intestines. The pain was terrible, but after having been burned over a thousand years and put back together with cleated ants, he knew he could tolerate it long enough to get down, long enough to get revenge on the bastard he held in his fist. After he managed to climb off the tentacle, he fell to the floor, warm blood trickling down the insides of his thighs.

Nearly insane with pain, Blaze lifted the crystal he had pulled out of the demon's head and smashed it to the ground. It cracked in a blinding light that sent the dogs whimpering and running away.

Blaze dropped his head to the ground and waited to die.

It didn't happen. In fact, he began to feel better. He propped himself up on his elbows and looked around. The dogs were gone, but Steph, still unmoving, sat at the table.

"Steph?" Blaze tried to stand, not knowing if his body would still work. His legs held his weight, so he took a step toward her. "Steph?"

She sat motionless, still holding her cards.

Blaze cautiously came closer. He reached out and touched her unresponsive figure with a finger. She cracked like glass and fell to the floor, shards dancing and bouncing on the stone with the sound of ruined crystal. Whatever this thing had been, it had not been Steph.

Blaze turned and looked around the room. There was nothing else here but the petrified squid-like body of the demonic thing he had killed. The sight of his own blood and insides dripping down the stone tentacle that had impaled him left him feeling queasy, but the rage that had built up inside of him since the now-dead demon had first started taunting him was still there, and he embraced it. He let the heat of his anger rise up and smother his pain and nausea. It fed him strength and resolve. He wasn't going to let this place beat him.

He stalked over to the newly created demonic statue and, with a roar of pain, anguish, frustration, and hate, he raised his foot high and began kicking at it.

The statue rocked back and forth until he managed to overbalance it, and then it toppled, shattering on the ground. The tentacle snapped off at the base, making a decent looking sword-like weapon. Blaze picked it up and hefted it. He shook his own blood and guts off the end of it, then looked around.

"Fuck you! Fuck you! And Fuck You!" he screamed, raising his new weapon high. "Who's next!"

ELEVEN

Blaze headed toward the back of the room, where the poker playing dogs had disappeared. The walls all looked the same, but he was sure they had gone back here. Did this place follow the same rules of the world he was familiar with? Obviously not, as he had already been killed and brought back to life. Twice now, really. He had been impaled and was now walking fine, although he was very reluctant to try to assess the damage by inspection.

Poking at the walls, he found nothing to indicate where the dog creatures might have gone. He walked out of the room and back into the slimy stone passage. He examined the door that had appeared in the middle of the impossibly long hallway. It hung, suspended by nothing, in the middle of the air.

Blaze peered around the back of it and found the door opened the same way as it had from the front, but it opened into a different room: a sitting room, replete with red velvet covered couches and overstuffed chairs. Coffee tables and bookshelves were everywhere. A hot pot of tea steamed in the middle of the room, next to two fresh cups, waiting to be poured.

"Please, Daniel, come in." The voice reminded Blaze of a British actor.

"My name is Blaze." He tried to stand proud and entered the room at the ready.

"*DANIEL.*" The word resonated through his soul, shaking him to his core. "That is your name," the voice returned to the gentlemanly tone, "no matter what you choose to call yourself. Please, come in and sit. I would like you to join Me for tea. You will never have better, I guarantee it."

A man strode into view. Dashing and handsomely swarthy, with neatly trimmed moustache and goatee, He wore a red and black smoking jacket and the finest black leather shoes. "This is what you expected, is it not? I thought about appearing as Morgan Freeman, but that would be a little gauche, don't you think?"

Blaze just stood and stared.

"Perhaps this is more what you expected?" The man waved his hand.

Suddenly Blaze stood surrounded in fire and brimstone with billions of souls around him, screaming in torment, and a giant demon overlord towering above in a bloody sky. The demon looked down, singling Blaze out with an unholy gaze. "*Daniel…*" The voice was like a nuclear explosion.

Then he was back in the sitting room.

"A little too dramatic?" The man wore a concerned expression as He looked at Blaze. "Please, have a seat. I won't ask again."

The implied threat was enough to move Blaze's feet. That he was in the presence of Satan, he was sure. Blaze sat in the nearest overstuffed chair and then looked down at his tattered clothing. He was covered in blood, slime, and demon ichor.

"Don't worry about the chair. The help here can do wonders with stains." Satan poured a cup of tea and brought it over, holding it out to Blaze with a polite smile on his face. "They've had a bit of practice."

Blaze dropped the hardened tentacle he had been holding. It hit the floor with a solid thunk. Shakily, he accepted the cup of tea.

Satan strode to another chair and seated Himself facing Blaze. He eyed Blaze, amusedly, over His own cup of tea as He took a sip.

Blaze sipped the tea, not wanting to offend Satan. After already experiencing the burning for a century that had only lasted a second, Blaze was leery of upsetting Him.

The flavor of the tea was indescribably wonderful, unlike anything Blaze had tasted before. It spread through him like the richest warm soup, warming his belly and spreading out to his limbs. His aches subsided, his wounds healed, weariness vanished. His thirst and hunger were slaked, his body was rejuvenated, and his mind became sharp.

"See? It is very good tea. My own special blend. I brew it with a distillation from the tears of suffering souls." Satan grinned wickedly. "But enough about Me. I want to talk about you, Daniel."

Blaze gaped down at the substance in his cup. Would the horrors in this place never end?

"No, they do not. Yes, I read your mind. If I can read your soul, why wouldn't you expect that I could read your mind? But that is neither here nor there." Satan took another sip of his tea before gently setting the cup down on its saucer.

"What is here, Daniel, is you. And you belong to Me. Your parents made a deal with Me, as they were dying. They had little to offer. Their souls were already coming here. But yours was not. So, in exchange for My promise not to immediately drag their souls down to Hell, and to let you have a good life, they gave Me your soul." He was matter-of-fact about the statement, businesslike.

"Yes," Satan answered Blaze's thoughts before Blaze could even form the words. "You were adopted, and your foster parents never told you anything about it. Why would they? Your biological parents were terrible, horrible people. You were so much better off growing up not knowing you were the love child of a notorious serial killer team. Besides, what if the relatives of their victims had come after you for revenge? You see, it was all for the best."

Satan eyed Blaze for a moment and let the revelations sink in. "I weary of My own voice. Gather your thoughts and use your voice. I will not interrupt. So few have the courage to actually speak to Me, I sometimes begin to feel…ostracized." He chuckled at his own joke.

"Even that fool dared not vex Me." He pointed to the tentacle on the floor. "I suppose I should have told it that I approved of its methods. It could be so *unbelievably* maddening with its imitation of human antics. Ah, well. Too late now."

"Did it have a name?" Blaze asked, surprising himself.

"No." Satan answered abruptly, apparently exasperated by the question. "Not in the sense you would comprehend. Next question."

Blaze hesitated, worried that he had irritated Satan.

"Come, come. Not asking questions will irritate Me more."

"Why am I here?" Blaze finally asked.

"Why my dear boy, I have not altered your memories. You walked through that door of your own free will. You tell Me why you are here."

"Because you took Steph."

"And you want her back. Why would you care what happens to some girl you've just met. You didn't know her for even an hour. Did she catch your fancy?"

Blaze frowned. "It…That thing," he pointed at the tentacle, "said she was my sister. That You owned her soul, too."

Satan nodded his head like a scholar considering how to explain a complicated matter to a child. "Mere tomfoolery meant to coerce you, I'm afraid. She is no more your sister than *that thing* was." He nodded back to the tentacle again. "Allow Me to show you."

Satan reached up and dramatically snapped his fingers. A puff of black acrid smoke appeared, and suddenly Steph stood naked in the room, between their chairs. A quick confused and panicked look crossed her face as she tried to cover herself with her hands

"Stop." Satan commanded her. Her features went slack and she stood motionless.

"Take the form of a dog," Satan casually said, sounding bored. Steph quickly melted into the shape of a large wolfhound.

"A lamp post."

The dog grew long and skinny and sprouted a light.

"A frog, a tree, a car, a donut…" Shapes quickly melted into one another, each becoming the next as Satan commanded. "…a doppelgänger."

Blaze found himself staring into a mirror. No. Not a mirror, a perfect copy of himself. When he moved, it moved, imitating him perfectly, but not mirrored. He raised his right hand and it raised its right hand. He leaned to his left, and it leaned to its left.

"Enough," Satan said, and Blaze watched as his twin melted back into Steph's form, standing motionless, naked, and waiting.

Blaze's mouth worked silently, unable to form the question for his brain, which was too confused to form it either.

A sly smile crossed Satan's face, and He said, "The Whore of Babylon."

Steph didn't change. At first. Slowly her bare belly swelled and she put a hand upon it, as if a mother lovingly feeling the child growing within her. She smiled at Blaze.

A horrid feeling overcame him. It was his child, his sin, that she bore, and that child would be the downfall of man. It was all his fault, and he knew it beyond a doubt.

The guilt of what he had done bore down on Blaze until he dropped his cup, spilling tea, and, still staring at Steph, shrank into himself, crying.

"You are in Hell, my boy. Nothing here is what it seems. Not even you." Satan looked at Steph and then back to Blaze. "Do you want her? I could give her to you."

At his words, Steph was no longer pregnant and Blaze's overwhelming feelings of guilt were gone. Steph began walking to Blaze, swinging her naked hips wide and pushing her breasts out as she moved forward. Her eyes locked onto his, holding them seductively as she approached.

Blaze felt lust unlike anything he had ever known before. It threatened to take over any reasoning he had left.

Steph kneeled in front of him and placed her open palms upon his thighs, gazing longingly into his face. She began slowly sliding her hands up and down his legs.

Blaze gasped at the intensity of her touch, unable to move, afraid he would lose control if he did.

It was all Blaze could do to tear his eyes away from her gaze to look back to Satan. "She's not human."

"No."

"But then…" Blaze tried desperately to ignore Steph, to focus his thoughts. "Why? Why was she there? Why did You take her through the door?"

"To get you to follow, of course."

"Why didn't You just drag me through the door the first time? Those things that took, they her tried to push me in."

"Of course they did. The operative word in your sentence is *tried*. They failed. So I sent another agent." He waved His hand at Steph. "Her method was much more effective. You walked in here of your own free will. Do you know how many people physically walk into Hell, let alone of their own free will? The statistical ratio would stagger you."

"So why am I here?" Blaze was having difficulty ignoring Steph's hot hands stroking his thighs.

"I wanted to collect on your soul early, as it were. While you still possessed a physical body to use. There are many things I would like to have you do for Me before you die, things that will change the world for centuries to come. In exchange, I will make your life a good one."

Blaze jumped as one of Steph's hands cupped his crotch.

Satan grinned salaciously. "And your eternity here the best one."

"What do You want from me?" Blaze pushed Steph's hand off his crotch. She grabbed his hand and held on to it like a desperate lover.

"Why, I thought I had made that clear. I want your services. I want you to do my bidding."

"What can I do that You couldn't already do?" Blaze tried to extract his hand from Steph's, but she just clutched at both of his hands.

"Nothing, of course. But then it would be Me doing it, not you. I want *you* to do it."

"But why?"

"Free will, of course. If I impose My will upon people, they have none. But if you impose your will upon people, you are using your free will to affect theirs."

"That sounds like an argument in semantics."

"Doesn't it though? But it is not, I assure you. By the way, I wanted to say that I am impressed with how fast you regained your composure and began speaking freely with Me. Most are never able to, no matter how civil I try to make our arrangements."

"What if I don't agree?" Blaze asked, fearing the answer.

Satan shrugged. "You can go home. You can go back to your apartment and your job explaining to people how to use their phones while they are talking to you on them. You can get married, have kids—or not. Whatever you choose. It's your life." He picked up his teacup and swirled it meaningfully while examining the contents. "But you'll spend your whole life knowing that I own your soul, and that no matter what you do, you will be coming back here." He sipped the tea, and a smile escaped his lips. "And you will no longer be the guest of a gracious host."

TWELVE

"I see you need some time to think this over." Satan took a last sip of His soul tea and stood up. "Stay with him, help him decide," He told the thing Blaze had been introduced to as 'Steph'.

"Give her to me," Blaze blurted out, surprising himself.

Satan smiled. "Of course, you may sate your appetite all you wish." Then Satan's smile vanished as He read Blaze's thoughts. "You mean you wish to possess her for yourself? Ah, I see. When I asked if you wanted her, you interpreted that as possession. Why should I do that?"

"As a gesture of negotiating in good faith."

Satan threw back His head and laughed. "You are negotiating with Me? Do tell what you offer in return, as a gesture of negotiating in good faith."

"My word that I will give your offer serious thought, not just dismiss it out of hand and deny you what you are seeking."

"And why would you want possession of this creature?"

"I—I don't know. It seemed like a good idea at the time."

Satan took a menacing step toward him. "I see into your soul, into your heart, and into your mind. I see that what you say is true. More than that, you have amused Me. A very rare feat indeed. I grant this gesture. You now possess this creature," He grinned slyly, "that you know nothing about."

He turned and walked toward a door Blaze had not seen before. Or that hadn't been there before. At the threshold, He turned back to Blaze. "I expect your answer within a reasonable timeframe. Send the creature to inform Me when you have reached your decision. Do not send it with your answer. I want to hear that straight from your own lips." He stepped through the door and vanished, and so did the door.

Blaze found himself alone with Steph. She was still naked, still kneeling at his feet, and still holding his hands, staring up at him desperately. He looked into her eyes. She met his gaze unblinking, unnaturally still, but with a pleading deep in her eyes, unlike anything he had ever seen.

"So…," he began.

She continued to stare at him.

"You are not human?"

"No, Master." Her voice was soft and breathy.

"And you belong to me now?"

"Yes, Master."

"Please don't call me that. It makes you sound like *I Dream of Jeannie*."

"As you wish."

"Please don't say that either."

She nodded her head in acquiescence.

"What are you?"

She cocked her head and looked at him quizzically. "I am whatever you want me to be."

"Are you a demon?"

"If you say so."

"What do you say you are?"

The confused expression intensified upon her face. "I do not say what I am."

"Work with me on this. What are you, when you are not being what your master wants you to be?"

"I…am waiting, for what my master wants me to be next."

Blaze sighed exasperatedly. "Get up." He waved his hand and she stood. "You're really not Steph?"

"I was Steph when my master required it of me."

"What are you now?"

"I am waiting for you to tell me what you require me to be."

The memory of the overwhelming lust he had felt for her mixed with the memory of the guilt he had felt when she had been pregnant. But she wasn't pregnant now…

"Can you put some clothes on?" Blaze asked, trying to reign in his emotions.

The creature materialized the nightshirt and jeans it had worn before.

"Thank you. What's your real name?"

"It is whatever you want it to be."

Blaze rubbed his face with his hand. "This is like 'Who's on First'. What does your master call you when He wants to summon you?"

"You are my master. You have not called me. I do not know the answer to that question."

"I mean Satan, what does He call you?"

"He does not. He just wills, and I come."

"Jesus! How—"

The room shook and Satan suddenly appeared in the middle of it. This time He did not look gentlemanly. This time He took on the appearance of a crimson half-man, half-goat with an angrily swishing, arrow-pointed tail.

"The only reason I suffer this offense a second time is that you blasphemed as well." His voice roared through Blaze's head even though the words were spoken with quiet anger. "I will not tolerate a third."

He pointed a finger at Blaze and smoke began to rise from Blaze's hands. Blaze cried out and fell to his knees in pain as charred skin appeared on the back of his hands in the shapes of crosses.

Upside-down crosses.

"A final reminder of where you are, and who you belong to." Satan vanished in a puff of sulfuric stink as Blaze fell to the ground, writhing in pain. The burns hurt much worse than he thought they should have, and he became sick to his stomach from the smell of his own charred flesh.

Steph, or the creature wearing that form, had remained motionless.

"Seen that before, have you?" Blaze gasped as he regained his feet. He looked at his hands and fought down a gag reflex as more of the acrid smoke reached his nose. He dropped them to his sides, pointedly trying to ignore them.

"No. I have never seen a human directly physically punished before."

Blaze tossed her a sideways glance as he gathered himself. "But people get tortured here. That's what this place is."

"They are not physically tortured. The people here are noncorporeal. They are souls."

"So what the fuck happened to me over there?" Blaze pointed to the stone remains of the demon that had impaled him.

Steph looked from the mess of blood and stone back to Blaze before replying. "I do not believe I could explain it in a way that you would ever fully understand."

"So…" Blaze huffed. Talking with this demon creature was an exercise in frustration. Probably yet another kind of intentional torture in this place, he thought. "What do we do now?"

"I am yours. We do whatever you wish."

"I wish you'd grow a brain and start talking to me like a real person."

The creature that looked like a twenty-five-year-old woman nodded its head in acquiescence. It froze, becoming unnaturally still, even for it, and a moment later it looked uncomfortable.

"What are you doing?" Blaze asked.

"Growing a brain. It is a bit unpleasant to actually grow an organ."

"You don't have any organs?"

"Not usually, no."

"What kind of creature are you?"

"I suppose you would call me a demon, but that is not really what I am. I am a creature of Hell. We are not like other things. Some came down from Heaven with Lucifer when he was cast out, others were created here."

"Wow! Talkative all of a sudden. That's better. Wait. You are growing a brain and talking to me like a human because I told you to, aren't you?"

"Of course. I must do your bidding. My brain is complete. What shall I do with it?"

"Uh…" Blaze was stumped. "Can you use it?"

"Of course."

"Well…I guess use it. Maybe it will help you realize the next time I tell you to do something metaphorically, I don't mean it literally. I'm just glad I didn't tell you to go fuck yourself."

"If you would like to watch me—"

"No! No, no. That was metaphorical." Blaze dropped into one of the chairs and looked miserably down at his burned hands. Smoke still rose from them. Steph stood and watched him, awaiting a command.

"Crap." Blaze dropped his hands over the sides of the chair's arms, where he couldn't see them anymore. "Now what do I do?"

The creature in the shape of a woman continued to stare at him, holding unnaturally still.

"Well?"

"Well, what?" The creature cocked its head.

"You are supposed to talk to me like a person, remember?"

"I thought that I had made a metaphorical-literal mistake and had corrected my behavior. I apologize."

"Are you real, in there?" Blaze stood up and tapped her on her forehead with his index finger. "I mean. Do you have any thoughts of your own? Or are you like an organic computer, you just do what you are told?"

"I… I have thoughts."

"Share them with me."

"All of them?"

"No. You would take that literally and we would be here forever. Literally. Give me your thoughts on whether or not I should accept this agreement with Satan."

"You should not."

"That was quick. No pros and cons? I thought you were supposed to talk me into it."

"I was told to help you decide. Those words were meant to imply that I should use sexual coercion to convince you that you wanted to accept it."

"Why haven't you done that, then?"

"Because Satan is no longer my master, you are. That order was issued before I was given to you."

Blaze thought about that for a moment. "I gave my word that I would consider His offer. I think accepting your opinion that I should not accept it would negate my part of the bargain. Do you agree?"

"I do."

"Then, please, tell me why I should accept the offer."

"You will live a very long, healthy, prosperous life. You will never want, you will never need, and, likely, all of your desires will be fulfilled."

"And I will have a pleasant stay here, after I die, for all eternity."

Steph did not answer.

"Right?" Blaze prodded.

"Doubtful. No stay in Hell is pleasant. Even were you to have a 'pleasant' stay, it would be for all eternity, and that, eventually, could be very unpleasant."

"I hadn't thought of that."

"No one ever does."

"Has He made this offer to others before?"

"Yes.

"How many?"

"Three million, nine hundred and sixty-four thousand, four hundred and twelve."

Blaze swallowed. "Did they all accept it?"

"No. Seven hundred and two did not."

"What happened to them?"

"They went home and lived long, miserable lives full of pain and suffering. Then some came here, where they have been enduring an eternity of suffering since, and others did not come here. I cannot say for sure what happened to them."

Blaze cocked a weary eyebrow and blew out a long breath. "So if I accept, I will mostly be happy and have everything I want, but if I turn it down, I will be miserable and have a life of pain. Why should I turn it down?"

"A long life of pain is less than a blink of an eye to a miserable eternity. Also, Satan is not known for bargaining with all costs clearly visible upon the table, so to speak. The tasks He would assign you start small and easy, but they grow into horrible things you will not want to do, but you will have no choice. You will rebel and be forced to do things anyway. Your reluctance will signify a breach of contract, and you will get to spend eternity being tortured in Hell."

Blaze was beginning to seriously worry there was no way out of this bargain, even before he made it. "But since He owns my soul, I will be tortured in Hell for eternity anyway."

Steph continued to stare at him.

"Well?"

"Well, what?"

"You have nothing to say to that?"

"I did not realize a response was requested. My response would be that faulty information leads to poor decisions."

"What faulty information."

"Satan does not own your soul."

THIRTEEN

"He lied to me?" Blaze was aghast.

"Of course He lied to you. He is Satan."

"And you didn't offer up this very relevant information sooner?"

"You did not—"

"Ask. Right. I saw that one coming." Blaze paced the room. "Je—" He stopped and looked down at the still-smoking black crosses burned into his skin. "I mean…Shit. Was He lying about the deal, too? Would He have given me what He promised?"

"I do not know His thoughts or intentions."

"What do you know? Fuck!" Blaze kicked at a chair. "Sorry! I just wish you were a bit more forthcoming with information. I'm sorry. I shouldn't have lost my temper like that."

"I have seen much worse."

"Yeah, I bet you have. Was the crap about my parents true? It sure felt real when He said my name was Daniel."

"Yes."

"All of it? They were horrible serial killers?"

"Yes." The demon, learning what Blaze wanted in conversation, made an attempt to be more helpful. "And they did offer your soul, but a soul is no one's to offer, except by the one it belongs to. So Satan could not accept it."

"Are my parents down here?"

"Yes."

"Do I want to see them?"

"I do not know your desires unless you tell me."

"I mean, would I regret seeing them?"

"I cannot predict the future." Seeing the look on Blaze's face, the demon continued. "But I suspect you would regret it."

"What about my real parents—I mean, my adoptive parents? Wait! Never mind. I don't want to know if they are here. I don't think I could handle that."

Blaze paced the room, putting his hands behind his back and then wincing and quickly bringing them forward again as the burns touched his body. "Steph?"

"Yes?"

"Are you sentient?"

The demon hesitated before answering. "Possibly."

"How can you 'possibly' be sentient? Either you are or you're not."

"I do not have free will. It is possible that were I to have free will, I would be sentient."

Blaze thought about that for a moment. "So you are a slave in every sense of the word."

"I do not understand your phrasing, but I believe I understand your question. So, yes."

"Steph?"

"Yes?"

"Can you get me out of Hell and out of this deal with Satan?"

"I do not know."

"Would you try?"

"I would not know how."

Blaze sat down again in one of the red overstuffed chairs. "I could use a drink of water."

Steph handed him one.

"Where did that come from?"

"I fetched it for you."

"From where?"

"It would be hard to explain in terms that you would understand. Consider it a pocket dimension."

"And what else is in there?"

"Everything. Nothing. It is eternal, yet it has no passage of time. It is not the same as that which you understand."

Blaze drank the water. It was cool and delicious, definitely out of place in Hell. He looked at his burned hand holding the glass. It all seemed surreal, yet too real at the same time.

"Do you hate Him?" Blaze asked.

"I assume you mean Satan, but the assumption is moot. I do not have feelings."

"If I told you to have feelings, would you?"

"I would emulate them."

"What is the difference between having feelings and emulating them?"

"I would respond appropriately for one experiencing those feelings, but I would not actually have them."

"How do we get you some actual feelings?"

Steph cocked her head. "Feelings are neurological responses. I have no nervous system, other than the brain you told me to grow. I have been attempting to use it as you have asked, to discern metaphors from literal, but I am finding it difficult to use it in this capacity."

"Use it for feelings. Grow a neurological system and get yourself some feelings. And when you are done with that," Blaze stood up and took a deep breath, "I grant you free will. I grant you free will and your freedom. You no longer belong to anyone. Can I do that?"

Steph stood still for a moment, and then Blaze could sense a change in her, but couldn't tell what it was.

"Yes," she finally said. "Yes, you can do that."

And then she was gone.

FOURTEEN

Stunned, Blaze stood in the silence for a moment, alone. He looked around the room, but there was no sign of Steph. He hadn't expected her to just disappear like that.

He thought about calling Satan and telling Him that he had made his decision, but the still-smoking crosses on the back of his hands gave him pause. The smoke from the back of his hands had stunk up the whole room. Blaze took another sip of water, hoping it would calm his stomach.

The water was still cool and refreshing, almost magically so. He poured a little over the back of one of his hands. The water sizzled and steamed, bubbling away where it hit the burn, but it lessened the pain and the wound stopped smoking. He quickly used the rest of the water on his other hand, the relief bringing tears to his eyes.

He sat the empty glass on the table.

What would Satan think about Blaze having set Steph free? He was sure Satan was not going to be happy about that, or about his own decision not to do Satan's bidding. He didn't want to see Satan again. Ever.

He would have to find his own way out of Hell.

He picked up the stone tentacle sword, just in case he ran into another asshole demon, and looked around the room. He had no desire to return to the never-ending hallway he had come from, so he chose to walk out the back door and into whatever kind of Hell it held.

It was a one-way trip. The door instantly vanished behind him.

Blaze found himself in a perfectly manicured field of yellow daisies under a crystal blue sky. The greens, yellows, and blues of life were all around him. Butterflies lazily flitted on the gentle breeze. Some were blue, others red or yellow. The field went on in all directions, for as far as he could see, with the exception of one moderately sized hill that blocked his view.

Blaze headed for the hill, resisting the temptation to swipe at the flowers with his sword. Glancing back over his shoulder he was horrified to see the trampled path he'd left behind him; an ugly swath of crushed flowers across the perfect world.

Then he noticed his breath.

It puffed out in little clouds, not of steam, but of exhaust. They reminded him of nasty diesel engine exhaust, and the harder he walked, the darker the puffs came out. Floating up above his head slowly, they collected in the sky to make an ugly brown cloud that tarnished the beautiful blue, leaving a visible trail marking where he had been.

When he stopped to rest, his pollution became less. It did not dissipate entirely, but it became less. The path he cut behind him did not recover any though. Each forward step destroyed more flowers, more beauty.

Blaze tried to step around the flowers, but they were as thick as any grass he had ever seen. It was not possible to move, or even just stand, without trampling the yellow splendor.

As he walked on, he heard something that sounded like faint crying. It grew louder as he approached the hill. Searching for the source of the lamenting, he noticed butterflies were beginning to congregate around him. A swirling cloud of rainbow leaves in a whirlwind, the butterflies flitted all around him as he walked.

And then he realized they were the ones who were crying.

Little blue butterflies, yellow ones, big red monarchs with black spots, yellow swallowtails, and more, all circled him, and he knew they were crying for the destruction of the flowers he tread upon.

But he had no other choice. He couldn't stand here forever. He had to move on.

He pushed forward and became aware of another voice crying. It took him a moment to realize it was his own voice he heard. Tears streamed down his face as his soul cried along with the mourning butterflies.

Blaze wanted to fall to his knees, to give in and wail with his grief, but that would just kill even more of the lovely flowers. And where would that leave him? Resenting himself, he tromped on, forcing his own loathsomeness upon the world around him.

Beginning to realize the nature of Hell, Blaze did his best to be undaunted by it, to try to recognize that this was not his fault, that he had not created this situation. He tried to draw strength from that and continue on. But deep down inside, he was sure Hell had been torturing people long enough that it would eventually find a way to bring him to his knees.

As he finally reached the base of the hill and began climbing its gentle upslope, he thought he spotted movement at the top, but it was hard to tell with the flitting of the weeping butterflies all around him.

The butterflies were so thick now it was becoming hard to see at all. They bounced off his hands and face as he walked. Several got crushed under his feet, as though they were trying to protect the flowers. One impaled itself upon the tip of his tentacle sword.

Nearing the top of the hill, he spotted the red flower. The only red flower in this infinite expanse of perfect daisies. It was a zinnia, the size and shape of a basketball. And it was rooted into the top of a trap door at the apex of the hill.

Blaze stood upon the top of the hill and looked outward as far as he could see, waving butterflies out of his face to get a clearer view. There were no other landmarks, no other breaks or changes in anything other than the brown cloud of his breath and the trampled path of dead flowers he'd made to get here.

There was nowhere else to go other than through the trap door.

As he bent to open the door, the butterflies' crying increased to wailing. Blaze pulled at the door and the roots on the red zinnia began ripping and tearing away, snapping like tiny ropes mooring the flower to life. The butterflies' began screaming, and the insects hurled themselves at him like kamikaze bombers, diving into his mouth, up his nostrils, into his eyes and ears.

He gagged on the feathery dust of their wings as they tried to suffocate him. In desperation, he began swinging the sword, trying to clear air enough to breathe. In a low swing, he felt the contact of the sword lightly against something and a shudder went through the whole world.

The butterflies pulled away from his face just in time for him to see the flowered half of the zinnia break free and fall off. He had accidentally cut it in two.

Butterflies fell to the ground around him in droves, sobbing in unbridled misery. All of the yellow flowers, everywhere, drooped their heads, bowing to the loss.

"Why?" gasped the disembodied red flower, lying on the ground next to its own wilting body.

"Why what?" Blaze wiped at the tears in his own eyes, trying to keep his vision clear.

"Why did you kill me?"

"It was an accident. I didn't mean to. I just wanted to open the door."

"But why would you want to return to Hell?" the flower cried. "It must have been so hard for you to get out…"

"Return to Hell?" Blaze was confused. "This is Hell."

"No. This is Purgatory. This is the world between Heaven and Hell."

"I didn't mean to hurt anyone." Tears ran down Blaze's face. "I just wanted to go home."

"All you had to do was ask, and the butterflies would have carried you anywhere…" The flower died.

The butterflies raged. They came off the ground in droves, their sorrow turned to anger. Swarming him again, they pulled at his hair, at his clothes, and began trying to suffocate him. Blaze swung the sword again, cutting furrows through the cloud of wings swirling in the air.

"I'm sorry!" he screamed. "I didn't know!"

The insects attacked mercilessly, driving Blaze back down the hill, hitting his face, flying into his mouth and nose.

Finally, in frustration and anger, Blaze attacked back. Instead of swinging the sword defensively he swung it offensively, attacking again and again at the densest areas of the swarm, swiping the butterflies out of the air, smashing them under his feet. He swung the sword until yellow butterfly ichor dripped off the end. He stomped and trampled his way back up the hill and to the trap door on top. He hacked at the remaining roots of the zinnia, ignoring the screaming protests of his winged attackers. The dead, severed head of the zinnia began calling and screaming for him to stop, weeping and begging that he not kill the roots too.

Blaze grabbed the handle and ripped the door open, tearing roots that trailed falling clumps of dirt. Red light, heat, and sulfuric stench belched out into the air around him.

He jumped in anyway.

FIFTEEN

Blaze fell into the heat and putrid stink beneath the trap door. A swirl of butterflies, unable to keep up with his falling body, dissipated in the wind rushing past him. The butterfly goo covering him darkened in the heat and then began to burn, peeling and tearing off in black flakes that were lost to the wind. He expected to find the red sun in the bottomless pit, but there was nothing. He fell an impossibly long way, twisting and turning in the void. If not for the rush of air going past, he would have lost the ability to determine which way was down. The heat, and the stench, diminished as he fell, or he was getting used to it.

Then he was on his feet, standing as though this was where he had been all along.

It was night. Stars shone brightly above, twinkling over a high desert area. Dark scrub brush blotted and mottled the ground around him. He found himself in the middle of an open area, on top of a hill, in a place that reminded him of New Mexico or Arizona.

Blaze took a deep breath, surprised the air was fresh, and relished the momentary calm. He was pretty sure this was just another place in Hell. He didn't think that last place was really Purgatory, either. Sure, his soul and his emotions had screamed out with all of the pain and destruction he had caused while trying to leave there, but that is exactly what Hell did to you, what Hell wanted from you.

Here, out in the night around him, the only thing that stood out was a faint glow beyond a hill. Just like the last place he'd been in, there was only the one thing obviously different than the rest of the surrounding landsacpe. Something that looked like a dark river meandered toward the glow and then away again, coming from, and going to it, as far as his eyes could see.

He hefted his makeshift sword over his shoulder, wishing he had a scabbard or something for it, and headed for the glow. The starlight was bright enough to easily avoid the bushes, but he still stumbled occasionally on rocks or holes. The night air was cool, but not cold. It felt good and refreshing. The sweet smell of mesquite and other things he didn't know drifted to him. He found the walk to be pleasant, not at all Hell-like.

But he kept an eye open anyway, watching for a bush to stab him, or to be growing naked women as fruit. He expected killer prairie dogs to come loping over the hill after him, or a meteor to suddenly appear in the sky. But nothing appeared. The night stayed calm.

As he approached the glow, still hidden by the hill, he heard the low thumping sound of loud music. Club music, perhaps.

A light appeared in the distance, and as he watched it move and grow closer, Blaze realized it was a car, driving toward the glow. The thing he had thought was a river was a road, and the car drove along it at a high rate of speed. It slowed as it approached the glow, and then it disappeared behind the hill.

Blaze waited, but the car didn't reappear on the far side of the hill. The glow must be coming from some sort of building, some place a car would head to. He wondered what kind of Hell someone was experiencing that would involve a car driving to a secluded destination in the middle of a nighttime desert, but he had seen enough of Hell's torments not to dwell on it long.

He resumed his march, switching his stone sword from one shoulder to the other, to rest his arms as he walked. The music became louder and recognizable as he approached. It was country music. And he could hear people.

Blaze stopped in his tracks. The people weren't screaming. They weren't crying or begging, they were…laughing.

In Hell? No, he shook his head as he thought about it, people don't laugh in Hell. Other things laugh in Hell, but not people.

But this sounded like people, not like the other things he had seen in Hell. But then, Steph had been one of those things, and she had certainly sounded human.

He couldn't take any chances. Nothing could be taken for granted in this godforsaken place. He chuckled at the thought. He really had seen a godforsaken place, and now he knew what one looked like.

Pushing through knee-high brush, Blaze finally crested the hill and looked down upon a country-western bar lit up enough to be straight out of a movie. Sitting isolated out in the middle of nowhere, off a desert road, it had a parking lot full of cars. A group of people stood outside the back door smoking cigarettes and laughing.

No one was screaming. No one was being tortured. There was no poor soul in the middle of the group begging for a cigarette or a light, or getting smoked themselves by a giant tumor.

Blaze stared down at the people. Was it possible he was no longer in Hell? The flower had said the trap door led back into Hell.

Blaze huffed at the thought; the flower had said. Since when did he trust what flowers said? Since the talking one in Hell, the one protected by butterflies that had tried to suffocate him. The flower that cried and begged…even after it was dead.

The flower must have lied. He had still been in Hell, and it hadn't wanted him to leave.

He felt weak in the knees. Had he really found the way out? Was he really out of Hell? Without even talking to Satan?

SIXTEEN

"Hey there's someone up there!" A woman's voice carried over the ambient noise of the music. The dozen or so people smoking behind the building all turned to look up at Blaze standing on top of the hill.

No point in standing up here looking stupid, he thought, and started down the slope. As he moved into the pool of light cast by the sodium floodlights on the back of the building, one of the guys commented to him.

"Must've been a mighty big rattler!"

Blaze frowned, confused.

"That thing you're carryin'. It looks kind of like a giant rattlesnake tail."

Blaze had almost forgotten he was carrying the sword. He held it out and looked at it in the light. With all the hardened suction cups on it, the tentacle piece did kind of look like a rattlesnake tail. With a wicked spear tip and nasty barbs on the end.

It still had blood on it. His blood.

"Yeah, it kind of does, doesn't it?" he agreed.

"What *is* that thing?" one of the women asked. She was wearing tight jeans and a red cowboy shirt with white frills on it.

"It's uh…a piece of art. I was holding on to it for a friend."

"Unusual art."

"Yeah, my friend has kind of a sick sense of humor. Hey, my car broke down a ways back. Where am I?"

"You are at the Waterin' Hole. This is the county line between Yuba and Chaffee counties. Everyone comes here out of Chaffee, because it's a dry county."

Blaze looked around uncomfortably.

"He's one of those," somebody muttered.

"No shit!" "Really?" Voices around him spoke up.

"You're in Oklahoma. Are you really one of them?" the girl in the red shirt asked in a hushed tone.

"Fuck this!" A man in a cowboy hat flicked his cigarette away and stalked off. He was followed by another guy nodding his head in agreement.

The remaining people all looked uncomfortable.

"You are not one of them, are you?" the woman asked again.

"One of who?" Blaze asked.

"Look at the back of his hands!"

"Oh, Christ Almighty. He's got to be one of them." Another woman dropped her cigarette and jogged back to the door in her high heels.

The other people started to murmur.

"He can't be." A man in a Harley Davidson t-shirt spoke up, but his voice was nervous. "That all stopped six months ago. There ain't been one for six months." The man kept shaking his head, like he was trying to convince himself. "It hasn't happened since Cthulhu showed up."

"Oh my God. That thing in his hand looks just like it!"

"What are you guys talking about?" Blaze blurted, confused. Cthulhu? Were they serious? They couldn't be. It had to be a name for something else.

"Jesus! He doesn't know! He *has* to be an escapee from Hell!" The woman in the red shirt got a panicked look on her face. "We gotta get out of here!" She was nearly screaming as she ran into the building.

Blaze heard a car start up in the parking lot, and then another. He turned to look. People were already leaving in a steady stream after being warned by the first cowboy to go in.

When Blaze turned back, he was the only one still outside the back door. Everyone else had gone.

"Shit." He had no idea what was going on, but it couldn't be good. Somehow they knew he had come from Hell, and they extrapolated that something bad was about to happen, so he probably should too. And he didn't even want to know what this business about Cthulhu was.

He had seen creatures in Hell that looked a lot like the classical depiction of that monster. He had a broken piece of tentacle in his hand that had come from one of them. And one of these people had recognized that it looked like Cthulhu…

As he tried to figure out what was going on, people began pouring out of the bar by the dozens. They were hurried and in a panic. Several stopped to point at him, often only to be jerked along by someone else in more of a hurry to leave.

The back door banged open and a surly looking man stepped out carrying a shotgun.

"You the one causing all the trouble?" he growled.

Blaze took a step back.

"If I did, I didn't mean to. I didn't do anything." Blaze started to put his hands up, but stopped when he realized that could be a threatening gesture with his weapon. Not to mention a possible confession of guilt.

"Pick a direction and start walkin'!" The man pointed the gun at him. "In fact, make that runnin'! I want you out of here, now!"

Blaze swallowed hard and nodded. He turned and headed for the highway instead of back up the hill. People in the parking lot panicked as he jogged toward them, slamming doors and squealing their car tires to get away. Horns honked as they tried to get others out of their way. Someone cursed as they, or their car, was bumped too hard.

Blaze considered following the road, but was afraid someone might take it in their mind to run him over, so he crossed the street as quickly as he could and kept the bar at his back. He wasn't worried about getting hit with a shotgun from this distance, but there was no telling what someone might have in their car and whether or not 'escapees from Hell' were shot on sight.

How had he become such a pariah? How had they known he had come from Hell? Then another thought crossed his mind. Six months. They had said Cthulhu had shown up six months ago. And he hadn't heard about it. So he must have been gone for… six months. Or more.

A flash lit the night and a loud explosion cut through the honking and yelling going on behind him. He turned to see a fireball coming up from the bar. Cars took off in all directions, no longer waiting for space on the roads. A couple of the vehicles headed right for him.

He dove out of the way as one failed to veer away from him. The car passed him, hit a bump, lurched upward, hit another, and then came down hard, sticking its front grill into the dirt and stopping. A series of small explosions from within the car signaled airbags deploying.

As Blaze recovered and picked up his makeshift weapon, he heard a voice coming from the car. It took him a moment to realize it was the onboard emergency service asking if the driver was all right. He heard no response.

Hurrying to the car, Blaze got there just as the driver started yelling back to the emergency service. "There are Hellhounds here! Someone said there was—" The man froze when he saw Blaze approaching. "Jesus Christ, help us all! He's right here! There's an escapee right here!"

Fighting with his door, the man screamed at Blaze. "Get away from me!" He opened the door and began stumbling into the night. "Get away!"

Shocked, Blaze stopped and let the man go.

Another explosion, a smaller one this time, came from the bar. Then another. Blaze turned to look. The man with the shotgun was silhouetted in the light of the flames. It didn't look like the man was pointing the gun at Blaze, but that didn't mean he wasn't firing at him, and Blaze wasn't sure he was out of range.

Blaze turned and continued running on in the direction he had been going. A shrill scream came from the bar, where there were still cars and people trying to leave, and Blaze risked a look. Smoke billowed up from whatever had exploded, the plume orange against the night sky, lit by flames. Then more screaming. Men and women.

This place was starting to sound a lot more like Hell.

Blaze readied to run on, not knowing where he was going, but knowing he needed out of here. Then two dark shapes appeared by the bar, darting on all fours, dog-like, between the cars. Much bigger and faster than dogs, their red eyes flashed as they wove through the wrecked cars, searching.

The man with the shotgun fired again, the flash of flame from the barrel revealing the grimace on his face. He tracked with his barrel and fired again. One of the creatures leaped over a car and Blaze gasped as he saw it rip the man's throat out.

"No!" Blaze yelled as he found himself running back toward the bar. "Over here! I'm the one you want! Over here!" He knew the words were true as he spoke them. The dogs were Hellhounds, come to drag him back to Hell. These people didn't deserve this just because he had walked out of Hell and into their parking lot. Anyone and everyone else would be collateral damage, mere chew toys for the Hellhounds.

One of the dogs spotted him, eyes blazing red with the fires of Hell behind them. It stopped, lifted its wide head to the sky, and gave a soul-shivering howl. The other hound joined in the battle cry and then, as one, they raced straight for Blaze.

Blaze held his charge, rage and frustration building up inside him. Satan had said he could go home, no matter what the decision, and now he sent Hellhounds after him? He hadn't even told Satan what his decision was yet! Everything Satan had said was a lie, or a truth twisted. That, on top of all the things he had already seen in Hell, was finally enough to push him past the edge of untainted sanity and into the brackish waters of madness.

He felt his concerns and worries slip away into anger, rage, and bloodlust. And he liked it.

As the first dog reached him, Blaze jammed the tentacle sword forward in a thrust that, combined with Blaze's strength and the Hellhounds momentum, speared into the beasts mouth, through its body, and out under its tail.

Blaze found himself lying on the ground with the Hellhound's teeth in his shoulder, his arm completely engulfed by the dead creature. He tried to pull the weapon out, but the barbs would not allow it to go backward. Struggling as the second Hellhound approached, he released his grip on his weapon and began worming backward to free his arm from the creature's mouth.

The jagged teeth snagged on the fabric of his shirt and down into his skin, pulling and tearing, anchoring him in place.

The other beast was nearly upon him, snarling with rage. Its eyes glowed with hate as it leaped at him—and was caught on the grill of a speeding Honda Civic.

The car bucked and bounced as the creature fell under the tires. Crunching bones were accompanied by squealing yelps. The car jerked sideways, threatening to tip over, and slid off the side of the road. The creature rolled three or four times before stopping. The flames in its eyes burned hotly as it tried to stand back up but was betrayed by a broken pelvis.

Blaze finally got his bloody arm out of the other beast's corpse and stood up. The mangled dog-thing, snarling and gnashing its teeth, drug its useless back legs behind as it pulled itself along with its front legs, determined to get to him.

Walking around to the backside of the beast he'd already killed, Blaze grabbed his weapon by the point and pulled it the rest of the way through the carcass, trying to ignore the gore and the smell. Repositioning the dripping stone sword in his hand, he met the still-crawling beast halfway and stabbed it through the brain.

The hatred in its eyes was the last thing to fade away.

SEVENTEEN

Blaze still stood over the beast, anger and rage dripping from his own soul, when a woman ran up to him. He looked around, feeling as if he was coming out of a daze. He had been on some kind of killing high when he attacked the dogs.

"You have to get out of here!" the woman yelled at him. Blaze recognized her as one of the women from behind the bar, the one in the red shirt with white frills. "Some people have stopped these things before, but the things that come next kill everyone! You have to get out of here or all these people will die!"

The woman desperately grabbed at his shirt. "Please! These people are my friends." She pointed at the wreckage and carnage behind her. "I don't know how many are already dead, but I don't want anymore. Please!"

Blaze nodded, the meaning of her words starting to sink in. "I have to get out of here, before …What comes next?"

She fumbled in her pocket and pulled out keys, pressing them into his palm. "Take my truck. It's the big red Ford over there." She pointed. "Just go! Go!" Near hysterics, she shoved him, trying to make him leave.

Blaze hurried toward the truck, moving back through the damage the two Hellhounds had caused. Several people lay on the ground moaning and crying, a few were obviously dead, more would join them soon. Was this really his fault?

He pushed that idea down. No, it wasn't. Satan would tell him it was. Satan would say he brought it on these people, but it was Satan who had done it. It was Satan's fault, no one else's.

Evil had done this.

Blaze reached the truck, unlocked it with the key fob, and then stepped up on the running board to get in. It was a spacious truck. He had never been in one this big before.

He put the key in the ignition and started it, feeling the truck rumble to life. The sheer feeling of power made him smile as he sensed the motor through his seat and the steering wheel. Putting the truck in reverse, he began trying to back out, amazed at how massive the truck was and how many blind spots it had. The mirrors on both sides stuck out over a foot away from the truck, making him feel like he was inside a longhorn steer.

After a couple of bumps into other cars and one near miss of a person, he finally reached the highway. He picked a direction at random. It didn't really matter which way he went, seeing as how he had no idea where he was. Oklahoma, they had told him.

He floored the accelerator pedal. The truck roared as the automatic transmission fought to keep up with how fast he wanted to go. He didn't even know which way he was going. East, the navigation device on the dashboard indicated.

East, he thought to himself. Kind of toward home. Kind of not. It was as good a direction as any. In the rearview mirror, he watched the glow of the fire fade into the night.

Six months… The thought floated through his mind. Had he really been gone for six months? The torture he had endured in Hell for saying God's name had seemed to last a century, but he had been told it had only lasted a second. Why couldn't the opposite be true then? What seemed to pass for a second for him could be a century out here. Or six months.

That was a whole new special kind of torture Hell could send out with him when he left. Assuming he was out of Hell.

Blaze was pretty sure he was out of Hell. This just didn't feel like Hell. There was too little misery, too little torture. The people who had been injured and killed back at the bar had had it happen to them too 'cleanly'. There was no long, drawn out, intentional causing of suffering like he had seen in Hell. And people stayed dead instead of being resurrected only to be killed again and again.

The truck jolted and shook. Blaze hadn't seen a bump in the road, but it felt as though he had hit a big one. A noise came from behind him and he looked in the rearview mirror just in time to see fiery red eyes shining at him.

Blaze slammed on the brakes. The truck's wheels locked up, skidding and bouncing along the pavement, giving off blue smoke in the red glow of the brake lights. The creature in the bed of the truck slammed into the back of the truck's cab and then flipped out, up and over the hood, and onto the road ahead. As it passed through the headlights, Blaze saw its awful bat-like body, leather wings, pug nose, wicked teeth, and blazing eyes.

A gargoyle? Blaze thought, as he took his foot off the brake and pounded the accelerator to the floor, speeding up to run it over. The creature stood up just as Blaze rammed the truck into it. Sharp claws screeched across the truck's hood, grating with the sound of metal being peeled back as the creature held on, preventing the truck from running it over.

It tried to spread its leathery wings, but the force of the wind plastered them against the grill like sheets slapping and snapping in the wind, preventing it from getting any leverage. The creature let out a throaty, shrieking cry, like the attack of a demonic hawk. It lifted one clawed hand up high and slammed it back down onto the hood, puncturing its claws through the metal for a better grip. Then it began pulling itself farther up, climbing its way up the front of the truck.

Blaze swerved the truck back and forth, trying to dislodge the winged monster. It scrabbled with its claws, but managed to get another, higher, handhold. Then one of its legs, swinging wide with the swerving movements of the truck, caught under a front tire. With a wrench of shearing metal, the creature was ripped off the hood and vanished under the truck with a jolt that lifted the tires off the ground and sent Blaze scrambling to regain control of the vehicle.

Stopping in the middle of the dark highway, Blaze turned the big truck around and raced it back toward the creature. The demonic thing flopped wildly in the middle of the road, one wing flapping madly, the other seemingly stuck to the ground. Blaze ran over the monster again. The impact sent the truck bouncing off the road.

Blaze turned the truck around and put the creature in his headlights. It was still moving, still dragging itself along the asphalt. Blaze pulled the truck close, keeping the thing in the headlights, grabbed his sword, and got out.

The creature made a mewling noise as Blaze stalked up to it. He stopped for a moment to look at the creature. Writhing in pain, helpless, it seemed little different than any other beast. He took pity on it by driving the point of the hardened tentacle through its left eye socket. It shuddered, sighed, and fell still.

It had blood all over its claws.

Blaze looked at the nasty black fluids leaking from the creature's wounds and realized the blood must be from the people back at the bar. Had he not left soon enough? Or had the creature stopped there to kill anyway? Or was he supposed to see the blood and lament the deaths of all those people and blame himself?

God, he hated Hell and everything to do with it.

He got back in the truck and drove on, wondering if there would be a round three of creatures chasing him from Hell and what they would be.

EIGHTEEN

The truck was nearly out of gas when Blaze pulled into the parking lot of the roadside diner. "Fanny's" was the name of it. He thought it was a joke at first, but after looking at it, Blaze decided it was probably old enough that no one had thought of the 'Fanny's: Eat Here and Get Gas' joke yet. Or maybe this was the place the joke had originated.

He parked the truck and left the keys in it. It wouldn't do him any good without gas, and he didn't have the money to buy more. As an afterthought, he checked the glove box. He found a small coin purse with a fifty-dollar bill in it. Not enough money to fill this beast of a truck with gas and get very far, but more than enough to get him something to eat at Fanny's.

He stashed his tentacle-sword in thick bushes on the little island of greenery separating the diner's parking lot from the motel next door. Leaving the grotesque thing in the truck might cause problems for the lady who had given him her keys, but carrying it around seemed like a bad idea, too. Hopefully city workers, and not kids, would find the thing and dispose of it.

As he walked into the diner, he expected everyone to turn and stare at the escapee from Hell, but no one did. The clinks of silverware on plates and quiet conversation filled the diner. There were enough bearded truck drivers to raise Blaze's hopes that the food would be good.

At the thought, his stomach growled loudly. He shook his head, slightly embarrassed, but after all, it had been over six months since he had eaten. Kind of. All he'd had in that time was the soul tea stuff Satan had given him. It had been wonderful at the time, but the source of it put him off, and the thought made him feel ill now.

"Seat yourself, Hon." A waitress, wearing a big smile and a pastel blue uniform, waved at him as she went by with two pots of coffee in her left hand and a pitcher of water in her right.

Blaze followed her into the seating area and picked out an unoccupied booth. He slid in across the sticky, red-glitter colored vinyl.

"I'll be right with you, Hon," the waitress said as she walked back by him with her hands full of someone else's food.

A television was on in the corner of the diner and several people were watching it intently. The sound was low but the big screen and the subtitles allowed Blaze to figure out what was going on.

'Cthulhu is moving!' the banner headline across the top of the screen proclaimed. In a side box picture, two talking heads were arguing over what it meant that Cthulhu was moving now, while on the other side of the screen an image of a giant, squid-like beast straight from Hell caught Blaze's attention.

The creature, easily the size of a city block, floated in the air above buildings that looked like apartment complexes. Its tentacles undulated in a sickening motion, as though it were floating under water instead of in the sky. The tentacles looked very much like the one Blaze had been using as a weapon. Then Blaze noticed the creature was hovering over his apartment building. Over his home.

Was this what Satan had sent to drag him back to Hell? Had it been waiting there for him to come home so it could grab him?

The image on the screen pulled out to show the shantytown of tents and motor homes of cultists that had taken up residence under the creature.

The subtitles showed the reports were talking about the creature finally moving, and then the video changed to a dark image recorded in the early morning, before sunrise, of the creature rotating and then floating off across the sky. Headed southwest, the subtitles read.

Southwest. That was opposite the direction he needed to go to get home. Was the creature coming for him? Was that thing going to be round three?

"Sorry, Hon," the waitress said as she returned to the table. "Please don't take this personal, but we get a lot of transients through here, and you look like you've been through the wringer. I can't serve you unless you can show me you can pay."

Blaze looked down at himself. He was covered in the black ichor from the Hell-spawned monsters and a little blood. His shirt was ripped, and he was filthy. He flushed a little.

"If you need food, I might be able to talk Sal into letting you work for it," she said gently.

"Maybe I should go wash my hands," he said embarrassedly as he showed her the fifty-dollar bill.

"That might be a good idea." She smiled and then her eyes flicked to the television and back to Blaze. "That sure is somethin', huh? I wonder why it's finally moving now? A lot of people are screaming it's the end of the world again, but that didn't happen six months ago, so why should it happen now, right?" Her voice sounded less sure than her words.

Blaze nodded silently in agreement.

"Why don't you go clean up in the bathroom, Hon, and I'll get you some coffee?"

"Thank you."

She smiled at him and walked away. Blaze scooted out of the sticky seat and headed for the bathroom. No one noticed his appearance; they were all watching the television and talking about whether it was God, the devil, or an alien.

When he came out of the bathroom, the waitress was waiting with a Styrofoam container in her hand, blocking his return to the main dining area. "Take this and go. Get out of here before someone kills you, Hon." She pointed to a side door emergency exit.

Blaze frowned in confusion, and then he saw the television's breaking news alert. The first escapee from Hell in six months had just happened in Oklahoma. There was video footage of the wrecked bar and the dead Hellhounds.

"Go."

"Thank you."

"Don't thank me, just go."

Blaze pushed his way out the glass door and quickly made his way to where he had stashed his sword. He felt silly digging around in the bushes to get it back, but he wanted it. Badly.

NINETEEN

Behind the service station, and hidden behind a clump of bushes away from the road and other prying eyes, Blaze ate the sandwich that had been in the Styrofoam container. It was fantastic. The best food he had eaten in as long as he could remember.

This wasn't the world he had expected to return to. He worried about what to do as he savored his meal. The world he knew didn't have a giant squid floating over his house, or gargoyles and Hellhounds attacking people as a routine occurrence. And people calmly watching it on television? How was that possible?

Was this really his world, or was he still trapped in Hell somehow?

As he finished his sandwich, it occurred to him there was perhaps a way to find out. He stood up and brushed the dirt off his clothing. Bracing himself for the worst, he called out, "Satan! I am ready to give You an answer!"

Nothing happened.

"Satan! I am ready to answer You!" He waited for a long moment before realizing he was supposed to send Steph to fetch Satan. But he had set Steph free. That wasn't going to work out so well.

"Hello, Daniel." A chuckling voice came from behind him. Blaze spun around, expecting to see the Father of Lies behind him, hoping He was in His smoking jacket and not in horns and tails.

Instead Blaze found a smaller, man-sized version of the squid-thing that was flying over the city on the television. It shot tentacles out at him, wrapping his arms to his chest, and pulled him in close so that it could stare into his eyes with its own sideways, slit-like pupils. It had sour, vinegary breath.

"The Boss is a bit upset with you for leaving without saying good bye," the creature warbled in his face. "But, lucky for you, He is also quite pleased with what you have done."

"And what exactly is that?" Blaze gasped, trying to free his arms, wishing he had been holding his sword when the creature had appeared.

"Why, you released the Beast, of course."

TWENTY

"Ah, Daniel!" It was Satan this time, and He was wearing the smoking jacket again as He received Blaze in the same study full of overstuffed red furniture. "So good to see you again. It was terribly crass of you to just leave like that without saying your farewells. I hope you've learned a modicum of manners since then and do not repeat that little faux pas."

Blaze sat stiffly in the same chair he had been in before, and fought the urge to drink the soul tea that had been set out for him. He was under the watchful eye of the creature that had captured him and brought him back, and he worried any motion he might make would end in something horribly painful.

"I understand you have come to a decision on our proposed arrangement. Are you ready to divulge your thoughts?" Satan seated himself across from Blaze and sipped at his own cup of soul tea.

"I respectfully decline your offer." Blaze's voice shook as he spoke the words, afraid of Satan's reaction. He was afraid of being back here in Hell. He was afraid of everything right now.

Satan sipped His tea again, His pinky finger carefully held in against the cup. "And you gave this serious consideration, as you agreed to?"

"I did."

"Prove it." Satan's eyes flickered with deep flames.

Blaze hesitated. "You can read my mind. You know I did."

"I agreed not to read your thoughts, do you recall? Therefore, you must prove it to me."

"How do I do that?" Blaze asked incredulously.

"That is your problem, Daniel. If you cannot prove it, I will assume that our 'good faith' negotiations were for naught."

"Well," Blaze cleared his throat. "You told…uh, the creature I called Steph, to help me decide, so I asked it the pros and cons of both decisions."

Satan's eyebrow went up slightly.

"Steph's explanation of the situation—of the proposed agreement, along with my own personal experiences, led me to the conclusion that you had proposed a lose-lose situation for me. No matter what choice I made I would regret it, possibly for all eternity. So, based upon the realization that I would regret either decision, I chose to make the one that I thought would least satisfy you. As my way of telling you 'fuck you' for trying to trick me." Blaze's heart pounded as he defiantly spoke the last sentence, sure that it would be his very last.

Satan's smirk was delightfully evil. The fire dancing in His eyes sparkled with glee. "Daniel, my boy, it has been a long time since someone had the nerve to say that to me. I appreciate your spunk! I do feel you did honestly consider the situation. And as per our arrangement, you are free to go home." He smiled wickedly. "Whatever may or may not be left of it."

"What does that mean?" Blaze asked.

Satan deigned not to answer, but stood up, continuing to grin. He started to leave the room, but then stopped and turned back to Blaze. "I believe that, when you come back, I may still grant you your eternity of enjoyment here. Out of gratefulness." His grin became impossibly wide and toothy. "I know that you have no idea what you've done, but it is just soooo delicious I cannot keep it from you any longer. Which is too bad really. I would have enjoyed waiting to see how long it took you to realize this was all your fault. But then, I wonder if you would have ever managed to figure it out. No matter.

"When you granted the creature you called Steph its own free will, you released the Beast. You have brought about the start of the End Times. Only a human could do that, and only of their own free will. I spent eons trying to put the idea in people's heads to free one of these creatures," He gestured at the demon standing at Blaze's elbow, "but they all were too repulsed or afraid to even consider it, or else they were too enamored with the idea of keeping it as a slave. You, my dear Daniel, have set forth a new type of creature upon the Earth. One that will destroy it. Thank you." He turned and strolled through an invisible door, his laughter fading away with him.

Blaze realized his mouth was agape and he slowly closed it.

Had he truly unleashed the end of the world by freeing Steph? How could he have done such a thing? How could he have known?

He could not have. He did not. This was Hell, he told himself. Don't trust anything or anyone.

"I am to return you to your home…" The creature standing beside him chuckled.

Blaze jumped. He had forgotten it was there.

"…or what's left of it."

TWENTY-ONE

In a whirl of shadows the demon creature that had brought Blaze home was gone. It had stayed only long enough to laugh at the look on Blaze's face when it left him standing in a pile of debris. The building had been demolished more thoroughly than if a tornado had hit it. Even the support beams were all shattered and broken into pieces less than a foot long. The plaster and glass were broken even smaller.

The buildings around it were smashed as well. Blaze stood in what would have been a clearing several city blocks wide, had it not been filled with shattered debris.

He turned in a circle, hoping the demon was playing a cruel trick, leaving him somewhere far from home, but he recognized the parts of the city skyline that were still standing. He was home.

His gut began to ache sickeningly when he recognized the smashed splotches of color that used to be the tents of the shantytown he had seen on the news. He did not see any bodies, but he couldn't bring himself to look for them either.

There was no giant creature floating in the sky above him, for which Blaze was very grateful. Now that he knew Steph was that creature, or at least that Satan said it was, he suspected the reason that it had been here, above his apartment building, was for him.

Had it come to smash him first?

The news had said it started moving for the first time after he appeared out of Hell. And it had been moving in his direction. Blaze had thought Hell had sent it to drag him back, but now he suspected it had come to kill him as a joyous exercise of the free will he had been foolish enough to grant it.

He looked at the ruin around him. There was nothing here for him now. There was definitely no shelter, and he doubted he could find any remnants of his apartment, let alone any of his personal belongings. There was no use staying here.

In a daze, he began walking, not knowing where to go. It took nearly ten minutes to walk out of the devastation. When he finally reached streets that had been untouched, the world took on a surreal appearance, like something out of a B-movie. Normalcy still existed on one side of the road, but on the other was an apocalyptic wasteland.

Cars still drove on the normal looking roads. Some police barricades had been set up to stop people from turning onto the roads leading into the devastation, but there was no yellow tape or guards to keep people out.

Of course not, Blaze realized, there was nothing to loot. There was nothing left.

A police car slowed down as it saw him walking out of the devastated area. He ignored it and walked on. The vehicle circled back and slowed down again as the police inside took a good look at him. Then the car pulled in front of him and blocked his way.

Two officers, a man and a woman, got out. Blaze recognized them as the police who had come the night he had been in Steph's apartment. Apparently they recognized him too. They arrested him.

The police station felt cold, like an institution. It had been built with economy in mind, not the comfort of the people in it. Blaze hated it. He felt bad for the police who had to be there every day. It had to suck the soul out of them.

Judging by the dour looks on the faces of the officers who had arrested him, it did.

Blaze, still in handcuffs, was being brought before the police chief for reasons the officers had not bothered to explain. They hadn't even bothered to read him his rights, just cuffed him and threw him in the back of the squad car.

Now, as they pushed him into the cold, heartless office, he wondered if he should mention the violation of his rights or just keep his mouth shut.

"This is the guy, Chief," the male officer said gruffly. Blaze thought he heard a bit of pride in the officer's voice, a bit of vindication.

"What guy?" The chief, a balding man with a wispy comb over, didn't even look up from his paperwork.

"The guy that lived in the apartment Cthulhu was watching," the female cop answered.

It took the chief a moment to register her words, but when he did, he looked up sharply. His mouth moved like he wanted to cuss and ask questions at the same time, but no sound came out.

The male cop pushed Blaze into a chair facing the chief. "We figured you would want to see him first, ask him some questions."

"Goddamn right I do!" The chief pushed his chair back and came around the desk. He sat on the corner nearest Blaze and leaned forward to look into Blaze's face. "What the FUCK is going on?" he growled through his teeth as loud as he could, his anger barely in check

"Sir?" Blaze raised his eyebrows.

The chief looked like he wanted to punch Blaze but refrained. "Do *not* play stupid with us. My people were out investigating a break-in and stumbled across you. Hours later, people all over the world, claiming to have escaped from Hell suddenly appear out of nowhere, only to be dragged back into Hell, or whatever, by God knows what kind of creatures. Then that thing," his hand pointed upward, "that alien, that beast, that devil, whatever the fuck it is, appears right over your apartment building. Everyone in those buildings said a girl was asking for you for days before that thing appeared, then that thing—"

He grabbed Blaze by the collar and pulled his face close. "Fuck this! You know what I'm asking about! You tell me what the fuck is going on!"

Blaze shook his head. "No. No I don't! I swear. I was gone! I was…I was in Hell! I just got back. I don't know what happened!"

The two cops began looking nervously around, afraid Hellhounds, or worse, might be coming for the man in front of them.

"No. It's okay, nothing is coming for me. They already caught me and dragged me back to Hell."

"Then why aren't you still in Hell?" the chief asked pointedly.

"Because Satan let me go."

The chief nodded, a quick bobbling of his head, his rage boiling in his eyes. "Used to be I got to lock people like you up for being fucking idiots that talked out of their asses. Now I gotta put up with you. Everyone's a fricking convert now. They're all still fighting over whose God is real, but they all believe in Hell. Fuck this. Lock him up, call the Feds. Tell them we've got that guy they were looking for."

"What? Why? I didn't do anything?" Blaze tried to stand, but hands on his shoulders pushed him back down into the chair.

"Tell that to the government boys who've been trying to deal with a giant Hell-spawned thing that floats in the skies and is immune to bullets. They got pretty goddam interested in you when that thing started shining some kind of supernatural spotlight on your fucking apartment for six months and didn't move. I'm sure they will want to talk to you now that it leveled the place a month ago and headed out to Oklahoma. Thank God for that, at least."

"Oklahoma?" Blaze looked at the faces of the officers. They didn't know he had been in Oklahoma. "If it really was looking for me, then why isn't it here, now that I'm back?"

"Who gives a fuck?" The chief flopped back into his chair and put his face in his hands. "Throw him in a holding cell and call the Feds."

The male officer grabbed Blaze by the arm and lifted him roughly. The female opened the door and held it. Just as they were exiting, another cop rushed in.

"Chief! The news says Cthulhu is headed straight back this way!"

"Fuck me! Call the feds, now! Tell them we've got this guy. I want him out of my city right the fuck now!"

The Feds had even less respect for Blaze's rights than the cops had. The first thing they did was inject him with something that knocked him out.

TWENTY-TWO

Blaze woke up in a hospital bed. He could feel the room vibrating around him. When he spotted the little round window, it occurred to him he had only seen windows like that on airplanes. He tried to move but found his arms and legs were restrained.

One of the machines hooked up to him must have alerted someone he was awake. A nurse came in and checked him out.

He tried to ask if he was on an airplane, but his throat was too dry. He couldn't speak.

The nurse, a petite lady who looked like she had never smiled in her life, held a small cup of water to his lips, pouring it even though he wasn't ready. The water seemed foreign to his mouth, like liquid had never been in there before, like it did not belong and his tongue didn't know what to do with it. He swirled it around, trying to moisten his mouth, but mostly just dribbling water all over his chin instead.

Two men dressed in suits entered the room before he was able to wet his tongue enough to ask his question. They looked even more stern than the nurse.

"Good morning," one of the men said in a way that made it obvious that this was neither morning, nor good, and he didn't give a shit. "It's time for us to talk. I hope you are in a talkative mood, because we have been informed that after all the drugs you've had in your system, the ones we use to make you talk could give you a heart attack, fry your brain, make you shit yourself, and make your piss turn green.

"Personally I don't care if it makes you grow another dick so you can go fuck yourself. You are going to talk to us one way or another. Understand?"

Blaze nodded.

"Good. Now then. Were you in Hell?"

Blaze nodded again.

"Can you tell us anything about Hell other than that you were there?"

"Like what?"

"Like what? Don't be an asshole. Everything. Anything. I want to know the colors, the smells, the things that made you feel tingly good all over, and what kind of animal your mom was fucking when you found her there!" The man was screaming in Blaze's face, on the verge of losing control.

The other man stepped forward and put a hand on his partner's shoulder, pulling him back away from Blaze.

"What my partner means," the other man spoke softly, but in a manner that Blaze actually found more threatening, "is that we want to know everything. From how you got there, to how you got out, and everything in between. No stone left unturned. Do you understand now?"

Blaze nodded and tried to speak, choking on his dry throat. The nurse put the cup to his lips again and he took another drink.

"Thank you," he said, but the nurse turned away, ignoring him.

He looked back to the men in suits and began talking. He told them of the dream in his apartment, of being pushed toward the door that opened out over a red sun, and of waking up again. He told them about falling back asleep and going back into the dream. He talked about hearing Steph crying and going over to help with the broken window and how Steph had vanished into that same empty space with the red sun.

The first man looked impatient, like he wanted to beat Blaze into talking faster, but Blaze did his best to tell the whole story and not leave anything out.

He told them about returning to the nightmare in his own apartment and then going into Hell himself. He did his best to remember all of the atrocities he had seen as he had discovered people trapped in their own private Hells. As he talked, he realized he was crying at the memories. Tears streamed down his face as he told them about the man fighting off the babies and the smartassed demon that had impaled him through the rectum with spiked tentacles.

His tears finally stopped, and he felt a hot rage slowly building up inside of him as he told about his meeting with Satan and how he had been told his true name was Daniel. He explained about Steph's advice that he was being set up and there was no good choice. He told about granting her free will and setting her free, then getting lost in butterfly limbo or Hell, or whatever it had been. The Hellhounds in Oklahoma, the gargoyle on the highway, going back to Hell to face Satan again, and being dropped off in the ruins of his apartment building six months after the whole thing had started.

When he finished, he laid his head back against the pillow, exhausted. It all seemed like one long nightmare.

The two men murmured to each other for a moment and then left.

"We looked into your story. You were adopted." The men, who Blaze assumed were FBI agents, had been gone for what seemed like hours, but had returned just as the nurse had finished feeding Blaze a disgusting substance that reminded him of Greek yogurt—if Hell had made it. "Your birth name was Daniel. Daniel Webster. Is that some kind of a joke?"

Blaze looked at them, confused. "What joke?"

"Daniel Webster."

"I don't get it," Blaze said.

"I believe him," the taller, more sinister partner said. "Kids these days don't know shit."

The other man continued to stare at Blaze for a long moment. Finally he said, "I don't envy you kid. If you have anything else to say about anything, anything at all, now is the time to say it."

"Especially if you think it will change things," the taller partner said. His face had softened and actually seemed to carry a hint of regret or sadness.

Blaze shook his head. "I told you guys everything I could think of. What are you going to do to me? Are you guys going to kill me? Because if you are, I would really like to see a priest first. I don't ever want to go back to Hell. I don't know what I have to do to avoid that, but it is pretty high on my priorities list."

"We're not going to do anything to you kid." The tall one smiled in what should have been a reassuring smile, but was sad instead.

"We're just going to help you have a nice long nap." The other one sounded more reassuring—until he picked up the syringe.

Blaze tried to struggle, but they injected him anyway. Whatever they injected him with was hot and spread quickly through his body. Then the world faded away in a warm fluff of black cottony goodness.

TWENTY-THREE

The rumbling woke Blaze up. It was an earthquake! The biggest he had ever heard of. The entire bed was shaking so hard, if he hadn't been strapped in, he would have fallen out.

Blaze panicked. He was inside a small, white, tube-shaped room of some sort, and he was strapped in. He was tied down to a form-fitting bed that looked just like...*just like...*

G-forces hit him and pushed him down into the chair, the blood rushed from his head and his last thought was, *just like an astronaut's chair.*

Blaze woke up with a vomit globule floating in front of his face. It just hovered there, not really spinning, turning, or moving, just floating. He knew it was vomit, because he could smell it.

As he looked past it, he realized there was vomit everywhere inside the tiny white tube he'd been encapsulated within. The vomit was soaked into his clothes, and, while it was not exactly dripping from the walls, it covered them with pus-like bubbles. Little bits and chunks floated in a fine mist of droplets everywhere.

This wasn't the eternal damnation he'd expected to be sentenced to in Hell. Everything else around him, the smooth white walls and clean white light, were too sterile.

Blaze tried to sit up and found he still couldn't move. He craned his neck and tried to examine his restraints, but he couldn't hardly see them. He tried to wriggle and kick, but he was secured too well. He couldn't move. He didn't bother screaming or yelling. He had already been to Hell; he knew those things didn't do any good.

Eventually he noticed a small timer on the wall. It was counting down and still showed an hour and a half to go until it reached zero.

Blaze settled in and waited to see what would happen, wondering if this was his personal Hell or if he was really on a spaceship with no gravity.

When the counter reached zero, Blaze's restraints released with a quiet click and freed him.

He gently floated up and inch or so without the restraints to hold him to the chair, but he held still and stayed quiet for a few minutes, feeling let down. That had been anticlimactic. He was pretty sure he was on a spaceship and had been speculating on being blown to bits in a fiery explosion. Or maybe crashing into the moon, or even just another launch booster firing.

As he pushed away from the seat, he found he had very little room, not much more than a large cylindrical one-man tent. He carefully tried to avoid the larger floating globules of puke. It was difficult, as they seemed to be attracted to him, like a magnet, drawing into him when he got too close. He finally took off his shirt and used it as a net to catch as much of the floating bile as he could.

Searching his new prison, he found he had access to another area through a small tube that made him feel like a gerbil in a Habitrail cage. He was disappointed to find the puke had worked its way in there too.

Free floating as he explored was fun, but would have been better if there was enough room to do anything more than spin like a log on a river.

Then the tube opened up into a larger area, one where he could actually stretch his arms out to the sides without touching the walls. He did so, and it was a near-joyous relief of movement. He found a small food storage compartment and a place that looked like a toilet, if toilets looked like they were made to have sex with. He was disappointed there weren't any view ports. He couldn't tell where he was going, or even where he really was.

He supposed it was possible he was still on Earth, but Blaze didn't think there was any way to sustain zero gravity for any length of time. Even short times would have been expensive, and who would want to waste money like that on him? And why?

As far as that went, who would want to spend the money to blast him out into space? And why?

Out of boredom, he set about cleaning all of the puke up. He found a water dispenser and had to stop and play with eating water bubbles out of the air first, then he went back to trying to clean off all of the surfaces in both compartments.

He found the food in toothpaste-like tubes, and the food itself to actually be paste. It tasted all right, but left quite a bit to be desired. Judging by the amount of food, he suspected he could survive for a couple of weeks, unless he decided to pig out on paste, in which case he guessed he could probably eat it all in a day.

He made himself dinner, playing with the Velcro and Bungee cords that held things on, or close to, the table. And then he spent some time screaming, just to hear the sound of his own voice. It was better than the nothing that filled the small prison. He found no radio, no television, books, or any entertainment of any sort.

About the time Blaze realized there was no reason for anyone to have previously built a ship like this one, a floating prison, and that they would have had to modify an existing one, he passed out from fatigue.

TWENTY-FOUR

Blaze awoke floating like an embryo in the womb. Stretching, his back felt great, but none of his muscles felt right. His movements sent him into a slow spin and the disorientation sent a wave of nausea over him.

Grabbing at a wall, he steadied himself and set about looking for areas that could have been sealed off to turn a spaceship into a prison. His best guess was that the toilets would be the farthest thing from the control center, so he went to the opposite side of his prison from them and began searching.

Now that he was actively looking for something, it was obvious a metal wall had been set into place and welded shut. Blaze poked and prodded at the wall, looking for weaknesses he could exploit, but found nothing he could do with his bare hands.

He began searching for anything that could be made into tools like a makeshift pry bar or a metal file. After twenty minutes he resigned himself to the need to destroy anything he could in order to get pieces that could be used to get useful pieces from other things.

He was just about to rip something that looked like a pair of lips off of the toilet when he realized he wasn't alone.

"Steph?" Blaze blinked, confused. Was he hallucinating? It wouldn't surprise him if he was, but he didn't feel that far gone yet. It had only been a day or so that he had been trapped in here. After his experiences in Hell, he would have expected himself to be able to hold out much longer. It wasn't like he was being flayed and burned alive like he had been in Hell. This did not seem nearly as hard to endure.

The figure before him nodded once, slightly.

Blaze tried to twist his body to match his orientation to that of Steph. She stood the way a normal person would stand on earth, feet planted on the wall, not floating at all.

He couldn't match her, and sent himself spinning. Twisting his head to look at her, he asked again, "Is that really you?"

"Yes," she answered.

"How did you get here?"

"I flew."

"Oh. I see." Blaze caught hold of the toilet and steadied himself by sitting and allowing it to suction onto him and hold him in place. "Where are we, exactly?"

"I cannot answer that in terms you would comprehend, but I think you would be satisfied to know our distance from earth is less than half of that to the moon, but we are in fact on a trajectory aimed for the sun."

"Oh. Well, it *is* kind of cold in here. It's nice to know it will heat up pretty soon." Talking to her in this place seemed surreal and he wasn't sure what to say. The more he thought about all of this, the more he thought maybe he *was* back in Hell. "Um, how long until we reach the sun?"

"About a year," Steph answered plainly.

"I don't think I have enough food for that long." He pushed himself away from the toilet and toward Steph. As he got closer, she reached out and caught him.

He looked down at her hand on his arm, felt her grip holding him. "You really are here. I thought I might be hallucinating." He smiled gratefully at the figure in front of him.

Steph steadied him, then pulled him in close and kissed him. Blaze almost resisted, but did not. He was so glad to see someone, anyone, and her especially.

She kissed him gently, then pulled him in closer and kissed him deeply.

Blaze felt himself start to react to the touch of her body and her kiss. He tried to pull away, but she pulled him closer and kissed him hard.

When he almost couldn't breathe, Steph let him go, and he drifted away, gasping, his hormones raging, and his mind confused. She was a creature of Hell, and he knew it. The memory of how he had felt when Satan said she was the Whore of Babylon flooded through him, and part of him wanted to pull away, to run and hide. But he also knew how good that kiss had felt, and how glad he was to have her here.

"I am glad that you are alive," Steph whispered. "Several times I was led to believe you had perished. I'm afraid I kind of lost control of myself at those times. I may have done some bad things. I may have hurt some people."

"What do you mean?" Blaze grabbed the wall, not sure if he wanted to pull himself back around to face her again.

"I was searching for you. When you did not come out of Hell, I went back in to find you. I tore the place apart trying to find you, but I could not." Her voice broke and he turned to look at her. Concern was deeply etched into her face.

"Is that how those people all escaped from Hell?" Blaze asked.

Steph nodded. "I'm pretty sure I made it worse for them. They were all hunted down and dragged back."

"I'm sure you made it better for them. You showed them that escape might be possible. You gave them a flicker of hope that Satan will never be able to extinguish."

"Perhaps that is why He did not try to stop me." She looked pensive. "He laughed the whole time I was there. I thought He was laughing at me, but now I think He truly enjoyed it.

"Enjoyed it? Why? Why would Satan like having you disrupt His mechanisms?"

"Because there really is no hope of escape for those souls. The hope will just make their suffering all the worse. And maybe because I relieved His boredom. He doesn't want to be there. He was sentenced there. All of us were. God wanted to make people earn their way back into His glory, but Satan felt that giving people a free will and then not allowing them to use it was not fair. He wanted everyone to be allowed back into Heaven."

"Wait a minute. You said all of us. You were cast out of Heaven?"

Steph hung her head in shame and nodded. "When Satan stood up with his opinion, I stood up to be counted with him. My punishment was to be cast down into the pit with him."

Blaze came close and cupped her cheek in his hand, looking her in the eyes. "You were an angel?"

TWENTY-FIVE

Steph and Blaze looked at each other across the table. Blaze had to hook his feet under the bars on the floor to keep from floating out. Steph did not. She was not affected by the lack of gravity, unless she wanted to be.

"I was something that you might have called an angel, but I do not believe that angels are what you would guess them to be."

"So you were an angel."

"I wish you would stop saying that"

"Sorry." Blaze played with his green tube of goo food, squeezing it up from the bottom, trying to get the last tiny bit out of it. "So... How have you been?"

Steph laughed, then looked surprised. Then she stopped and looked demure.

"Are you all right?" Blaze asked.

She nodded, but did not say anything.

"Do you want to talk about it?"

Steph stared at the various tubes of goo on the table. She hadn't touched hers. "I am going through some changes," she said slowly. "Things I do not really understand. Things I thought I understood when I was on the outside looking in, but now that I am on the inside, they seem very different."

Blaze nodded sagely. After a moment of silence, he tried a tube of orange goop. He grimaced at the not-quite-carrot flavor and asked, "Would you like to elaborate upon that?"

Steph looked up at him. "I have become enamored with you." She watched closely to see what his reaction would be.

Blaze carefully put down his tube of goo, wondering if his life depended upon his reaction in the next few seconds. It might not be wise to reject a demonic creature from Hell that has just expressed love for you.

He swallowed.

"I thought you didn't have feelings." Blaze kept his voice as neutral as he possibly could.

"Then why would I have kissed you just a few minutes ago?" Steph's voice rose a bit, and it made Blaze nervous.

"Um. I thought you were trying to act human so that I would feel more comfortable in your presence?" He winced as he said it. He knew something was wrong with what he had said, but he didn't know what it was. He always said the wrong thing when dealing with women.

Steph looked crestfallen. "Only trying to act?" she murmured.

"Oh. No! You were very convincing! I mean, look at what a seductress you have been in the past! Obviously you are very convincing!"

Steph's eyes flashed and he knew he had said the wrong thing again.

"Look." Blaze reached out across the table and tried to take her hands, but she pulled them away. Awkwardly he pulled his own back and tried to meet her eyes. When she finally let him meet her gaze, he realized something was different about her. Something behind her eyes. Something that hadn't been there before.

He could not say how he knew, or how he could tell, but he could. "Oh my God, Steph. You…you have a soul."

TWENTY-SIX

"I do not have a soul. I have a nervous system. I have a brain. One that you told me to grow. After you granted me free will, I was going to eliminate them, but I discovered that understanding how people act when they are experiencing feelings and actually experiencing them are very different things. I decided to keep it, to see what it did, to learn from it. Instead, it became a new master I am slave to." Steph's face was impossible to read, so many emotions flickered across it constantly.

"If you are a slave to it, you can get rid of it."

"I do not want to!" Steph showed her anger and confusion for the first time. Regaining control, she sat back in the chair and repeated quietly, "I do not want to.

"I used to have a semblance of feelings, a shadow, an imitation, just enough to make me think I understood them, just enough to allow a modicum of enjoyment out of torture or success, or to find humor in others' failures or misery. Now, I do not know what those were. Guidelines? Rules to help me accomplish what I needed to accomplish? Why would a creature such as myself have any feelings at all? I realize now that I did, and that confuses me more. I thought I had none. But now…now I have them, and they are so much more intense than I ever thought they could be!

"My joy is limitless, my sorrow without depth, and then, when I see you, I have both, at the same time! How is that possible?"

"That's what feelings are, Steph. That's what we all deal with."

"It doesn't feel like free will. It feels like chains and restrictions, manipulations and influences. It feels like I do not truly have control of myself."

Blaze nodded. "That is what being human is. Why else do you think there are so many stories about temptation, lust, love, betrayal…? Isn't that how you were trying to take advantage of me? I mean, when Satan told you to. You were trying to get to my lust, my protective feelings, anything you could to overwhelm my rational thoughts so that you could manipulate me."

Steph nodded. "I knew that then, but I understand it differently now. Before it was just funny, like watching a cat playing with a mouse, but now I realize how overwhelming it must have been for you." She started crying. Tears welled in her eyes and broke free, floating away in the lack of gravity.

"Steph? How human have you made this body? You seem very…overwhelmed by physiological reactions. First you kissed me like you were…well, like you were horny as hell, and now you're crying real tears…"

Steph wiped at the tears. "I made it as real as I could. I— I wanted you to like it." She sniffed and then looked at him. "Do you like it? I can change it. I can be anything you want me to be."

Her desperation pulled at his heart.

"You know I like it. Didn't you originally shape it to fit my expectation of what was attractive?"

She nodded again.

"Well then, trust yourself. You know I am attracted to that shape."

She waited a moment before speaking. "But what about me?"

"What do you mean?"

"I need to know if you are attracted to *me*." Her eyes desperately sought the answer in his own, looking back and forth between them.

Blaze took a deep breath and held his hands back out across the table, waiting to see if she would hold hers out and meet him halfway. It took a long time for her to decide to put her hands out and hold his.

"Now, you have asked me a question, and I am going to answer it, but you need to listen to my answer, do you understand?"

Steph nodded, but Blaze wasn't convinced.

"I need you to understand that who and what you are has nothing at all to do with who I am or what I think about you."

She tensed up and tried to pull her hands back, but he held on tight, looking into her eyes.

"This is the hard lesson we humans all go through as adolescents. We spend the first part of our lives so sure of ourselves, sure our parents and our siblings love us, sure we can do things, sure we won't get hurt… Then we start to go out into the world, to meet other people, and a lot of them, sometimes most of them, don't like us. And it hurts." He squeezed her hands reassuringly. "It hurts a lot. We start wondering what's wrong with us, why are we different, why don't we fit in, why aren't we good enough? Some of us have it even harder. Some of us know there is something wrong with us, we know we are different, and then we expect people to treat us differently. We look for it even in people who weren't treating us differently.

"Are you still listening to me?"

Steph did not look happy, but she nodded.

"Good. I hope you understand what I am trying to say to you. Because you are different. You know that, I know that. No one else in the world would know unless you told them, but you will probably still expect them to, because you know it." He saw the look in her eyes and knew she was running out of patience for his answer, and that she thought she knew what he was going to say.

"I like you Steph." He looked deeply into her eyes. "I am very attracted to you. And I think you need to realize that the very fact that I know what you are, or rather what you were, and that I am still sitting here talking to you like this, without running and screaming, worried that you are going to rip my head off and eat me," he nudged her and tried to get her to smile, but it didn't work, "says a lot about how I feel about you. But the truth is; I don't know you. Not really. I know nothing about you. But I want to. I want to get to know you."

By the look on her face, he knew he had stopped stalling the answer just in time. He could tell she wasn't sure if she liked his answer, but it wasn't the one she had been afraid of hearing.

He waited a minute to let her think about what he had said and to give her a chance to digest it. She continued to hold his hands and look into his eyes as she thought.

Finally she spoke. "Thank you for being understanding and honest with me. I—I needed that. The emotions… They overwhelm me, and make it hard to think properly. But I like them. I want to keep them. After millennia of being cast out, it feels so good to be back in the light."

"Back in the light?" Blaze asked.

"This is what I remember it felt like to be in the grace of God. Not exactly, but similar. The joy, the feelings, the wanting, the desire to please…" She leaned forward slightly, her eyes still searching his. "I want to please you…Blaze."

He hesitated. It seemed so strange to hear her say his name. Hadn't she used his name before? It didn't feel like it. It gave him a thrill to hear her say it.

She saw the emotions flash across his face, and her own face turned worried. "You do like me, do you not?"

Blaze blushed. "I do, but I really don't know you."

"Well, can we get to know each other better?"

Blaze waved his hand at the little room around them. "I have nothing more pressing to do." He grinned. "Nowhere else I have to be."

"Can we start with sex?" Steph's eyes gleamed as she asked the question.

Blaze raised his eyebrows.

"I cannot stop thinking about it!" Steph laughed. "I mean, I have had sex before, but, I never…*wanted* to. I never expected my own pleasure out of it. I have always…faked it."

Blaze laughed. "I can't promise you won't still be faking it. I'm not exactly the world's greatest lover."

"It—it is not so much the physical pleasure I—I need the closeness. The comfort, the companionship."

"Those I am pretty good at." He grinned at her, but his humor was lost on a newly-human being.

She stared at him blankly.

"Are you enjoying my company right now?" he finally asked her.

She hesitated as she considered. "Yes. I think so."

"See? I'm good at it." He grinned again. She still did not respond.

"We need to work on getting you a sense of humor."

TWENTY-SEVEN

The sex was unlike anything Blaze had ever imagined. Steph had started off slow and nervous, her feelings affecting her in ways they never had before. Once she became more comfortable, Blaze became nervous. She was wild beyond anything he had ever experienced, and he had to keep cautioning her that his body was not like that of a malleable shape changer from Hell that could withstand most any damage.

The zero gravity was interesting, too, once Steph allowed it to take her body as well. Blaze thought perhaps his favorite position was one he dubbed "the helicopter." When they moved fast, he could hardly bear the overpowering sensation, but when they went slow it became one of the most sensual and erotic things he could imagine.

On every pass by each other's face, they would slow for a kiss, then continue on in rotation. When he climaxed, Blaze was sorry it had ended.

"I wish that moment could have lasted forever," he told Steph as he held her tight.

"Me too." She looked wistful as she nestled her head against his. "I have never experienced a moment like that. One where I lived in the moment. I had never fully understood that expression until now. I will remember and treasure that moment forever."

They floated in silence for a while. Finally Blaze asked, "So what do we do now?"

Steph frowned at him. "What do you mean?"

"Well, for starters, and for reasons I don't understand, I'm on a spaceship headed for the sun."

"That would be because of me, I am afraid," Steph said. "When the men who took you figured out I was trying to find you, they put you on the ship and sent you away from Earth, hoping I would go as well."

Blaze nodded. "And you did. And I am glad. But I don't have enough food to actually reach the sun, and even if I did, I would just burn up when I got there. You can't stay here with me. I mean, I guess you could, but I wouldn't want you to burn up in the sun."

"I would not burn up in the sun unless I allowed it to happen," Steph told him. "The mortal world holds no dangers for me."

"You mean, you can't die?"

"Not unless I choose to."

Blaze frowned. "But…I don't know how to say this without being indelicate, but didn't I kill a…being just like you when I was in Hell?"

Steph nodded. "Yes. Quite surprising that was, too. But we were not in the mortal world. We were in Hell. And you were not a normal denizen of Hell. You were a mortal man who walked into Hell of his own free will. Admittedly Satan tricked you into doing that, but you did it nonetheless."

"Why would He do that? Why did He want me in Hell?"

"To get you to agree to do what He wanted. He has very little influence on your world directly, so He has to get others to do it for him. By tricking you into coming into Hell, He showed it to you, He frightened you with it, and He manipulated you so that you would want to take His deal."

"But I did not."

Steph grinned at him. "No you did not. In fact, you did something He never expected by granting me my freedom."

Blaze looked at her thoughtfully. "Are you sure?"

"Sure about what?"

"Sure that He never expected me to set you free? What conditions had to be met to set you free like that? Who could have done it?"

Steph looked surprised. "Well. Only a human could have truly set me free."

"And the only way for that to happen was if Satan 'gave' you to a human?"

Steph nodded.

"How many times has Satan given you to a human before?"

"Thirty-two."

"And how many times has He given others like you to humans?"

"I do not know, but many."

"So I offer the idea that Satan has been doing this for a long time, hoping that a human would set one of you free."

"But in the past we have had to return to Satan as part of the bargain."

"But in the past, no one offered you free will either. Could Satan have told someone to do that?"

"No. That would have been against the rules."

"Whose rules?"

"Why, God's rules, of course. They were imposed upon us when we were cast out of Heaven."

"And did you know this loophole in the rules existed? Or was it something Satan had worked out on His own?"

"I did not know it existed."

"Then how did you think the 'Beast' would be released from the pit? That is what Satan told me. That I had released the Beast from the pit."

Steph pulled away from him, hesitating before answering. "I only knew that it had to be done by a human." She turned away, and, ignoring the lack of gravity again, sank to the floor. "So you know I am the Beast?"

"Are you?"

She did not answer. Blaze twisted in the air and grabbed at the wall, trying to pull himself into a position where he could look at her.

"Steph? I have seen you as a lot of things. A demon, a companion, a seductress, and now as lover and as a friend.

But I have never seen you as the Beast. Are you sure you are the Beast? Or is Satan manipulating you now, too?"

She looked back at Blaze, tears in her eyes.

"Do you or do you not have free will?" He held her eyes with his as he maneuvered himself next to her. "Because if you do, you don't have to do anything you don't want to. He can't make you. He can trick you, manipulate you, lie to you, and force you to endure things you don't want to, but Satan cannot make you *do* anything anymore. Am I right?"

"You are right." She sat up straight, and Blaze was jealous he had to hook his feet in so as to not float away. "No one can make me do anything I do not want to."

"So," Blaze added, "what is it the Beast is supposed to do? Besides bring about the end of the world?"

Steph shook her head. "That is it. I do not know details."

"Easy peasy, then. Just don't bring about the end of the world, and you are not the Beast."

"But I am. I was set free. And God prophesized it."

"Just because God said it would happen, doesn't mean He said *you* would do it. Did He tell you to do it?"

"No."

"If He did, would you have to?"

"Only if He rescinded my free will"

"Then that would not be you doing it. That would be God doing it and using you as a tool. You are not the Beast unless you choose to be."

Steph wiped tears off her cheeks and then threw her arms around Blaze in a tight hug that made him gasp for air. After a few minutes, she whispered in his ear. "So what do we do now?"

TWENTY-EIGHT

"Are you sure this will work?"

"Unfortunately, a side effect of having emotions and a nervous system is that I never feel completely confident about anything anymore." Steph frowned at him. "But it will work." She kissed him and then her body began to change shape into a more squid-like form.

She enveloped him within her body, wrapping herself around him, creating a pocket of air around his face.

"Can't you just teleport me? Like the other demon did?" Blaze asked. "That seems much less risky than flying through space wrapped inside your body."

A mouth formed next to Blaze's ear. "If I were to teleport, I would have to first go into Hell, and then come back out where we wanted to be. I do not know about you, but I do not ever want to go back into Hell again."

"I thought you already had been back. Isn't that how those people escaped?"

"I was looking for you. And now that I have found you, I do not intend on letting either of us go back there."

"Oh. Right. And how are you going to make sure my soul doesn't go back. You going to make me become a priest? How does that look on my soul's report card? A priest who really, really, enjoys fornication with a former denizen of Hell."

"It would not be the first time." Steph sounded like she did not enjoy what he had said.

"Well, how many of them made it into Heaven?"

Steph did not answer.

"See?"

"There is always Purgatory," she finally said.

"I have been there. It's just another kind of Hell."

"Well, it is not supposed to be Heaven. But at least you can still get to Heaven from there."

"You can't ever get to Heaven from Hell? Then what is the point of all the torture?"

"Penance."

"Why would I ever repent if I could never leave? What is the point? Is it really torture just for torture's sake? Is God getting off on it in some sick and twisted way?"

Steph hesitated at the airlock she had just been prepared to blow open. "I hadn't ever considered that. I just assumed it was permanent, until Judgment Day."

"And what happens on Judgment Day?"

"God judges you, of course."

"And…?

"And if you are found worthy, you join His kingdom."

"And if you are found unworthy? Back to Hell forever?"

"No." Steph's voice became solemn. "You cease to exist."

"So the people in Hell could still end up in Heaven, when Hell ceases to exist?"

"I believe that is correct. Yes. Yes. That is what will happen."

"So that is why Satan wants to bring about the end of the world, then. So He can get back into the Kingdom of Heaven."

"That seems a plausible motive, yes." Steph kicked out the door with a large tentacle, and the air whooshed out in a swirl of ice crystals.

"Oh, shit," Blaze muttered.

"Are you injured?" Steph's concern was immediate.

"No. I just figured out why you *are* the Beast."

"Why?"

"Because you are immortal. Because you will not die. You will live forever."

"That makes me the Beast?"

"If the only reason you're not killing everyone is because you love me, then yes. I am mortal. I will die. Maybe not now, maybe not soon, but I will. And then what will you do? Mourn me quietly, weakly, like a human would? Or rage out against the world? Destroy it all in your anger, your frustration, and loneliness?"

"I hadn't thought of that."

The flight home was boring, not at all like Blaze had imagined. The little ship he had been in hadn't even made it as far as the moon, so there was no cool Star Trek moment where they flew past all of the planets in the solar system. They just flew through the blackness back to Earth.

Fortunately, Steph was much faster than the spacecraft had been, and it only took them about fifteen minutes.

"I would go faster, but I am afraid of the effect it would have on your physical body," she told him.

Re-entry into the atmosphere was a blinding flash of white as Steph forced her way through the air at an unbelievable speed. Then they were standing on the ground.

The echoes from the concussion of a sonic boom still carried away from them as she released Blaze from the cocoon of her body and resumed her usual human shape.

Blaze took an unsteady step, getting over the shock of the landing and readjusting to gravity.

"Why didn't you move that fast when you were looking for me before?" he asked. "You just kind of floated like a balloon."

"I wanted to be visible, so that you could locate me, if you were trying, and I did not want to panic the humans any more than necessary."

Blaze laughed and hugged her.

They stood in the middle of a grassy park, somewhere in England, Blaze thought, based on what he had seen of the geography of the Earth as they came in.

"Why here?" he asked.

"Why not? The whole world is ours. We can do what we want."

Blaze smiled. "For a little while, maybe. But if we do too much like that, it will be noticed, and then they will all be after us."

"What does it matter?" Steph asked. "If we have decided to bring the world to an end anyway, who cares what everyone else thinks?"

"So you have decided then?"

"I do not know that I decided so much as that the decision was made for me. I do not know how I could choose otherwise. How long could I remain aloof among the humans after you have departed? How long could I blend in and pretend to be one of them? How many lovers could I take before I found no emotions to go with their company? How long until utter despair sets in and I destroy the world out of a rage and desire to destroy myself?"

"You've never had this problem before? When you were in Hell? Or before that, when you were in Heaven? How did you face looking into the abyss of eternity then? How did you cope?"

"I did not have the feelings then, for starters. But also, I was not alone, there were many others, all like me, and we did not have free will, so to speak. We did not face the possibility of having nothing to do, no interests, no desires. It was all laid out before us, and we were told what to do, and we were content."

"Do you miss that? Do you regret having freedom and free will?"

Steph did not answer.

TWENTY-NINE

"Are you happy living like this?" Steph asked Blaze as they sat and watched television. The show was banal, and not worth their time.

"Of course! I love you! This has been the best two years of my life."

"I do not mean that. I know you love me. I mean, are you happy just living like this—like completely normal people, with normal lives, and normal problems."

"Um." Blaze did not know what to say. "I thought that was what you wanted. To live like a normal human being."

Steph looked away.

"Hey, honey. What's on your mind? Tell me what you're thinking about. Please." Blaze got up and walked over to where Steph was sitting on the loveseat. He sat next to her and put his arms around her. "Hey. It's me. If you can't talk to me, who can you talk to?"

"No one, Blaze, and that's the problem. I thought I would have you, and I thought that would be enough. It was all I really wanted, and now I feel selfish. Now that I have you, I feel like it is not really enough. I feel like I need more. I...I feel like I need more people, I need to know more people. I feel like I need to do something, something productive and useful, and...I do not know."

"You feel like you're better than all of this?"

She gave him a dirty look.

"Not like that," he hastily corrected. "I mean, like you were meant to do more than this. That the job at the gas station is okay, but you were meant for a higher calling? That there is something important that you should be doing, if only you knew what it was?"

Steph nodded. "That's really close to how I feel. It amazes me how often you understand me." She laughed a little as she got up, got a tissue and dabbed at her eyes.

"I have had feelings longer than you have, Sweetheart. I have gone through most of them before. And most people have that feeling. If not that one, then one of inadequacy. I find it hard to imagine you with that one though." He smiled slyly at her.

"What do I do about it then?" she asked.

"What do you want to do about it? What do you feel like you want to do that would make this better?"

"I do not know.'

"Well, what is it about our life, or what we are doing, that bothers you the most? What can we change?"

"I feel like we are keeping a big secret that everyone should know. I feel like we need to tell the world that Satan tried to destroy them, using me, and that He will try again and again. I feel like it isn't fair that so few humans are allowed to know for sure that God exists, and yet they are required to behave as though He does."

"They don't have to behave as though He exists. They just have to live a good, respectful life. Right? Treat each other like you would want to be treated and all that. Right?"

Steph looked at him sadly and shook her head.

Blaze's jaw dropped. "Well then how are you supposed to know which religion to pick? Which God to worship? Is it really okay to suicide bomb? Will you really get a bunch of virgins in Heaven? Crap, Steph, don't leave me hanging here!"

"No, it's not like that. It is more that you have to believe in Him and live your life for him."

"So it really *is* God's work to be a suicide bomber?"

"Of course not. That is the doings of men, for their own purposes."

"But how are you supposed to know when other men are manipulating you?"

She didn't answer.

"Which god do you have to believe in? The Jewish god, the Christian? Muslim, Buddha, Shiva, Zeus? Which is right?"

"It doesn't matter so much which religion you follow as that you give yourself over to His higher power."

Blaze thought about that for a moment. "By giving yourself over to God, you mean giving up your free will?"

Steph pursed her lips at that. "I suppose it could be looked at that way."

"So, it bothers you that everyone has to believe in God, but no one is really given any evidence to make up their own minds with?"

"Well, some people get evidence. You did."

"I most certainly did. Sex with an angel is nothing to be ignored."

"Fallen angel."

"Says you. I think you are heavenly."

Steph blushed.

"So you want to put the word out that God is real?" Blaze asked.

"Yeah, I think I do."

Blaze sighed. "I knew you were going to turn me into a preacher. I just knew it."

THIRTY

Thirty-five years later, Blaze, now known as the Reverend Daniel Webster, stood at his pulpit and looked out over the massive congregation filling the stadium. His wife, Steph, sat off to the side of the stage in a comfortable folding chair. Blaze looked out over the fifty thousand people gathered to see if he would make good on his promise.

He looked up at the morning sky, just beginning to turn pink and blue from the rising sun. He could not have asked for a more glorious Easter morning, or a more perfect day for the world to end.

He and Steph had worked long and hard for today to happen, and now that it was here, he found himself strangely calm, strangely subdued. He had thought it would be a relief to finally get this over with, to get it finished. Instead, it felt like most any other day.

He looked to Steph and smiled. She smiled back. It had been a good life together. She had worked hard at being human, at helping him stay on the path of good and righteousness so that neither of them would ever have to go to Hell again. He had to admit, he didn't think he could have made it without her. Not just to here, this place, at this time, but as a human, trying not to go back to Hell.

His first inclinations had been to drown himself in alcohol and cry about the things he had seen and experienced in Hell. Her first inclination had been to rip him apart, literally, for being weak. Together they learned, they taught, and they worked to make the world a better place.

The television cameras were on him, and he chuckled to himself at the absurdity of waiting for a commercial break to end before he announced the end of the world. The red lights on the cameras came back on, and he knew he was about to speak live to over a fourth of the world's population.

It had been a long road to get here.

They had fought accusations of being a cult, they had fought government regulations, and they had fought the police and people who recognized him as someone who had escaped from Hell. They had been accused of being Satanists, of being the False Prophet, and of being the Second Coming. They had fought so many things to reach this pulpit, and Steph and he had stayed side by side every step of the way.

The only regret he had was that they couldn't have children. Steph had grown ovaries, a uterus, and all the organs needed to be fully human, but a pregnancy had never naturally occurred. Blaze and Steph assumed it was because she wasn't "only" human. She had offered to split a part of herself off, to reproduce asexually, and to try to incorporate his DNA into it, but they both agreed that had a risky side to it and smacked of something God would not have approved of.

"Greetings brothers and sisters, and welcome to this glorious day." He smiled as he waited for the applause to end.

"For thirty years now, you have been listening to us preach. We have preached about a great many things, but we are most famous for two things specifically. First, as you all know, we started a new religion. A religion of hope, of love, of acceptance. A religion of charity, kindness, and giving. A religion devoid of ostracism, racism, sexism and every other "ism" we could throw in there."

The crowd cheered at his joke.

"We have also preached about the coming of the end of the world. We have even gone so far as to name a day and a time. And that, I suspect is why you are all here." He smiled sadly. "I am sorry to say that we, indeed, picked this time and date pretty much at random." He listened to the people mutter.

"Oh, no. Don't get me wrong. We weren't making it up. It is still going to happen. You see, we have something the rest of the world doesn't have. We have our hands on the button. We have our hands on God's button. God built this world with a self-destruct button. I don't know why. I don't understand why. But I do know that He did.

"I also know that He put this button in Satan's hands and allowed Him to play with it like a child. Allowed Him to push at it, pull at it, twist it, turn it, poke it, and prod it until He could figure out how to make it work.

"The thing was…Satan could not make it work. He had to have someone else do it for Him. And He picked me." He listened to gasps from the audience.

"Yes, it is true. I was picked, not by God, but by Satan. And I was chosen, not to save the world, but to destroy it. But—" He waited until he could be heard over the crowd.

"But Satan did not take something into account. Something very important: I am human. I have free will. As do each and every one of you. I make my own choices. God gave me that ability, and I will have it until such time as God takes it away again. And when He does, it will no longer be my choice. It will no longer be my doing or my fault. It will be His. It will be His Will.

"Now you should be asking yourself, 'What is he saying? What does that mean to me? Why do I care? What should I do?' but you are not. You are not because you have already written me off as a nut job. You are wondering when I will admit the world won't end today. You are wondering when you can start laughing at me, and move on.

"You can do that at any time. You have free will. You can choose to ignore me. And that is exactly what I did. I exercised my free will, and I chose to ignore Satan.

"To my surprise, He was all right with that. And that confused me. It worried me. Because, after all, He is Satan. Why would He be content with me not doing what He wanted me to? Well the answer was obvious. It was because I *was* doing what He wanted me to. He had manipulated me. He turned me into the trigger that would end the world.

"And that was where He made His mistake."

Blaze glanced over at Steph and she smiled brightly at him. They had talked about this for thirty-five years. There were no more surprises between them.

"His mistake was He put the button in my hands. He wanted me to play with it. To twist it, turn it, push it, pull it, prod it and see if I could make it work. Well, I can. You hear me Satan? I can! But I *won't*.

"I am a human being, and I have free will, and I exercise my right to not do your bidding. I choose not to end the world!"

Laughter broke out in the crowd again and someone signaled to him that they were getting ready to take another station break in thirty seconds.

"Instead, I choose to rebirth the world. I choose to give, to you all, the hope of an everlasting world, by teaching you what the button is, and how not to push it.

"Most of you know my wife, Steph." Blaze gestured with a wave of his hand, and she stood up and began walking over to the podium. "What most of you do not know is that she is a demon from Hell."

Laughter broke out again throughout the crowd, and he got a signal that break was in fifteen seconds.

"Steph. I love you. Please, show them who you are."

Steph began to swell in shape and size, ballooning up into the sky until she had retaken the Lovecraftian form she had used before, when others had called her Cthulhu, thirty-five years earlier.

"Do you still want to change the channel? Do you still want to go to commercial?" Blaze asked with a satisfied gleam in his eye.

"This is the button Satan gave me to play with! This is what God gave Satan to destroy the world with!"

People were panicked, screaming and pushing their way out of the stands, pushing past each other, trampling each other trying to get away.

"Steph! Please come back down!"

In the span of a heartbeat, Steph stood beside him again, fully clothed and looking exactly as she had before.

"Now many of you may remember her from thirty-five years ago!" Blaze had to yell to keep his voice over that of the panicked crowd pushing its way out of the stadium. "Many of you may have believed, or wanted to believe, all of the governmental cover-ups saying it was all a hoax, that it never happened.

"Well I am here to tell you it was real. It was the end of the world. And I stopped it. I put the end of the world on hold for you. For all of you. To give you all a chance to put yourselves in order, to get yourselves right before God, so that when you die, you can go to Heaven, not to Hell.

"I have seen Hell. I have been to Hell. You don't want to go there." Blaze continued his speech although people continued to panic and run. He knew the cameras were on him. He knew they were recording, and he knew he had the attention of most of the world by now.

"What does it take to get into God's good grace? I have no idea. What does it take to go to Hell? I don't know that either. What I do know is that God had the audacity to create a system like this, where we go to Heaven or Hell, but then didn't bother to hand us a rule book. Oh, some people claim he did, in the form of the Bible, or the Koran, or whatever, but those were all written by people. And any parts that might have been accurate have been tampered with, by people. And Satan has been manipulating people since they first walked upon the earth. There is nothing there, in those words, that we can trust.

"That is why I established a new religion. One of peace and love. One based on rules that we can all see, that we can all understand, rules that hopefully will allow us to get in to Heaven.

"And if they don't, well, then to Hell with God. What is the point of free will if you get punished for using it and rewarded only by not using it?"

"Steph and I are imposing our free wills against those of God and Satan. We are choosing to not destroy the Earth as They wanted, but to preserve it, as *we* wanted.

"I promised you the end of the world today, and I say I have delivered it. The world is no longer as it was. I have the proof right here," he put his arm around Steph, "that God and Satan are real, and we are the proof that God truly did grant us free will and that we can use it to alter the plans of God himself!"

Red splotches appeared on Blaze's chest. His eyes went wide, and he fell backward into Steph's arms.

THIRTY-ONE

"No!" Steph screamed. "No!" More bullets hit her, but they did nothing to her demonic body. She cradled Blaze's head in her hands. "Talk to me! Blaze! Talk to me!"

Blaze's head lolled to the side, and he went limp, his eyes already lacking the gleam they'd had moments before. Lacking the love for her she had seen and treasured every day. Lacking the life she needed him to have, so that she wouldn't be alone.

"Blaze!" Steph shrieked, her emotions overriding her thoughts more than they had in over thirty years. She shook his shoulders and slapped his face, but she knew he was gone.

"Damn you!" Steph's demonic voice shook the stadium as she stood up, holding Blaze's body in her arms. "Damn you all!"

She folded herself around him, cocooning his body with hers, as she changed form and grew again into the giant behemoth, rising up above the stadium. People, streaming like ants out of an anthill, running for their cars, scattered below her. She shook with an unholy rage that vibrated through the very Earth itself.

The highways around the stadium were already jammed and traffic was stopped. Cars began plowing through the medians and down the shoulders to get through the stopped traffic. People got out and ran, carrying children in their arms, leaving invalids behind to fend for themselves.

Steph was now the Beast, with writhing tentacles, great squid-like eyes, and millennia of demonic hatred. It roared in anger, frustration, and loss. The sound, unlike anything heard on Earth before, killed people who were too close, broke windows for miles, shook buildings, and killed the television feed.

The destruction was apocalyptic. The Beast wiped out the entire stadium and everyone in it within a second. The giant, writhing demon smashed and beat at the ground with enormous, razor sharp tentacles. No longer moving as though drifting in water, the Beast was quick, darting faster than the eye could follow. In less than a minute, everything in a mile radius had been smashed; every car, every house, every tree. Within two minutes, every living thing, human, animal, plant, and microbe, had been specifically sought out and killed with ungodly speed by infinitely sharp, spiked tentacles. By the time ten minutes had passed, Seattle was nothing more than a flat spot on the coast, and the government had scrambled attack aircraft that had been waiting in preparation ever since the first time the Beast had appeared, forty years earlier.

The first nuke added little to the destruction. The second and third made sure nothing would live there again for a very long time.

None of the nukes had been needed. Steph had already turned back into human form and was crying over her beloved Blaze in the center of the destruction she had wrought.

She was ashamed that she had lost control and killed all of those people. She was…repentant.

As she sobbed over Blaze's body, she prayed. She prayed that Blaze had been good enough to have gotten into Heaven, so that he would never have to see Hell again. She prayed for the people she had killed, that they would find peace in the afterlife. And she prayed for forgiveness.

She prayed for her own forgiveness. She did not ask to be kept from Hell. She did not ask to come back to Heaven. She had no delusions of ever going back to Heaven; she knew what her punishment was when she had been cast out millennia before.

But she prayed for forgiveness for having betrayed the humans who had come here to see her and Blaze, who had come to be taught about salvation, but instead had been given destruction. She prayed for their families who would grieve for them, and she prayed for the people who would now forever live in fear of such a thing happening again.

She was nearly completely human when the first nuke hit. And she died that way.

THIRTY-TWO

"Where are we?" Steph asked quietly.

"Purgatory." Blaze smiled at her brightly. "We are in purgatory."

Steph hopped up and down like a little girl and then threw her arms around him and kissed him deeply. She broke free of the kiss, laughing, and spun herself around in the yellow flowers that surrounded them.

"I've been here before," Blaze said. "The butterflies don't like it much when you do that." Then he noticed her passing hadn't trampled the flowers, hadn't smashed them into the ground or left a dying trail of them behind her.

He took a cautious step and found that the flowers did not crush under his feet either, but rather they seemed to move out of the way. He reached down and touched one. He could feel it. He could smell it, touch it. It felt as though he could pick it, but he had no desire to do so.

Steph leaped upon him again and they fell backward into the flowers with her arms around him, kisses covering his face. When she finally stopped, she stood up and called out, "Thank you God! I know I did not deserve this chance! I won't disappoint you!"

"What do we do now?" Blaze asked

"We make sure that when Judgment Day comes, we are worthy, so that we can stay together forever." She kissed him again.

"How do we do that?"

"Well. For starters, we go see who else is here, and what we can do to help them."

"Will there be time for kissing?" Blaze asked.

"There will be time for kissing from now and through all eternity!" She cried with unbridled glee and kissed him again as the butterflies found them and began to circle.

"How do we find someone?" Blaze asked, eyeing the butterflies nervously. So far none had tried to fly into his mouth or up his nose.

"We fly!" Steph looked as though she intended to leap up into the air.

"Okay. How do I fly? Can you teach me?" Blaze asked.

Steph looked confused. "I—I cannot fly."

"What?"

"I cannot fly." She furrowed her brow. "I cannot change shape either!"

It was Blaze's turn to be confused, and then Steph's eyes went wide.

"Oh, Blaze! Do you see what this means? I am a soul! A real soul, just like you!" She threw her arms around him again, tears streaming down her cheeks as she squeezed him tightly.

Blaze held her close for a moment. "I know what to do," he told her. "I can't believe I know something about this place that you don't!"

He kissed her again and then scooped her up in his arms. "Take us to someone who needs help, please," Blaze asked the butterflies, remembering that last time he'd been here the red zinnia had told him all he had to do was ask.

The butterflies swarmed around them and picked them up, lifting them above the flowers and bobbing them along toward an unknown destination.

Steph giggled with excitement.

ABOUT THE AUTHOR

A Colorado native, Sam Knight spent ten years in California's wine country before returning to the Rockies. When asked if he misses California, he gets a wistful look in his eyes and replies that he misses the green mountains in the winter, but he is glad to be back home.

As well as being Distribution Manager for WordFire Press, he is Senior Editor for Villainous Press and the author of five children's books, four short story collections, three novels, and nearly three dozen short stories, including two media tie-ins co-authored with Kevin J. Anderson.

A stay-at-home father, Sam attempts to be a full-time writer, but there are only so many hours left in a day after kids. Once upon a time, he was known to quote books the way some people quote movies, but now he claims having a family has made him forgetful, as a survival adaptation.

He can be found at SamKnight.com and contacted at Sam@samknight.com.